GIRLS ONLY!

DAILY THOUGHTS FOR YOUNG GIRLS

OTHER BOOKS BY KAREN CASEY

Each Day a New Beginning
Promise of a New Day
If Only I Could Quit
Worthy of Love
In God's Care
Notes from the Heart of Recovery
A Life of My Own
A Woman's Spirit
Keepers of the Wisdom
Daily Meditations for Practicing the Course

GIRLS ONLY!

DAILY THOUGHTS FOR YOUNG GIRLS

BY

KAREN CASEY

HOLY COW! PRESS • 1999 • DULUTH MINNESOTA

Text and introductions, ©1999 by Karen Casey
Cover woodcut by Rick Allen

Grateful acknowledgment to Patricia Hoolihan, Jan Zita
Grover, Lisa McKhann and Marian Lansky, who provided
invaluable editorial assistance.

Library of Congress Cataloging-in-Publication Data

Casey, Karen.
Girls only!: daily meditations for young girls / Karen Casey
p.   cm.
Summary: A collection of 366 daily meditations focusing
upon problems and situations involving familial relationships,
friends, and strangers, suggesting affirmative responses, and
featuring inspirational quotations from exceptional women
such as Helen Keller and Eleanor Roosevelt.
ISBN 0-930100-92-1 (pbk.)
1. Children—Conduct of life Juvenile literature.
2. Affirmations Juvenile literature. 3. Self-reliance in children
Juvenile literature. 4. Children—Religious life Juvenile
literature. (1. Prayer books and devotions. 2. Conduct of life.)
I. Title.
BJ1631.C37   1999
158.1'28'08342—dc21   99-40711
CIP
First Printing—Fall, 1999
10 9 8 7 6 5 4 3 2 1

Published by Holy Cow! Press, Post Office Box 3170, Mount
Royal Station, Duluth, Minnesota 55803. Distributed to the
trade by Consortium Book Sales and Distribution, 1045
Westgate Drive, Saint Paul, Minnesota 55114.

ACKNOWLEDGMENTS

So many people have contributed to my journey as a writer that the task to name them all is too formidable. But I do want to tell my husband, Joe, that without his sense of humor and easy ways, I would not feel as free to sit and await the "Spirit's" message.

Patricia Hoolihan has been an invaluable editor. She has managed to take my thoughts and, where needed, clarify them. Her sensitivity to the message and my philosophy has made *Girls Only!* sing with great resonance.

Jim Perlman, publisher of Holy Cow! Press, deserves praise too. He took a rough manuscript and, through very specific suggestions, vastly improved upon it. To him I owe a significant measure of gratitude.

And I want to thank all my friends in recovery who have been my strength and my hope for nearly a quarter century. You are never far from my thoughts and I love you.

Girls Only! is dedicated to the many young girls in my life. Hayley, grandniece number one, first comes to mind. She is a delight, and makes me smile when we spend time together. Emily comes next. Her sizzling personality is accentuated by a shock of red hair; she keeps me entertained. Anna Lisa and Jenna, full of fun and spice, never allow for a dull moment. The same can be said for Kaitlin, Jessica, and Katie. And then there's Allie; though not a niece, she is very special in my heart. Through each of them I have revisited the joys and sorrows of girlhood. Each journey is bittersweet.

A Note to Parents

I first thought about writing a book for young people three years ago. When the idea came fully formed into my mind, I was startled. I was sitting in a board meeting, more or less listening to the discussion, when my inner Spirit screamed, "Listen up!" Within minutes I was taking notes as fast as possible on the ideas flooding my mind. I left the meeting knowing that I was moving as a writer, at least temporarily, toward a new audience.

At first I felt as if I needed to justify this move. Although I had taught school and worked with young people in many capacities over the years, I did not have children of my own. How could I presume to know the struggles of a young girl today? All I had to do was reflect on and share a bit about my own troubled youth, though, and people understood why I wanted to share my girlhood experiences.

I didn't invent low self-esteem, but I certainly suffered from it as a girl—well into adulthood, as a matter of fact. My struggle began in elementary school, where I never quite fit in, never felt good or cute or smart enough. I was not alone. Although I didn't realize it then, I was like many other girls in my classes. And little has changed. Girls, and boys too, are filled with fear about who they are and if they will ever succeed. What a sorry state of affairs that we help each other so little to feel whole!

My intention in this book is similar to the intent in my other titles: I want to foster hope and willingness in young girls to believe they can make the changes needed so they feel like they belong and have purpose. Self-assurance is wonderful. Some say it's a gift, like grace. Perhaps that's true for some, but it can also be fostered and nurtured by words about who we are and what we can be. The messages here are ones I wish I had heard as a young girl; I think they would have made my journey very different. If a girl you know needs encouragement, I want to help her. It's never too late to help her change directions.

If you have a young girl in your life to whom you want to offer a helping hand, I wish both of you well. Perhaps discussing some of these meditations with her will offer both of you some insights.

We cannot do too much to help each other heal. Listen to your heart, hope for change, and seek help from the Spirit in your daily life. Offer your help to someone else.

Please know that my thoughts and prayers are with each of you as you make this journey to help someone young and in need of wise counsel.

–Karen Casey

Dear Reader,

I hope you are helped by the meditations I have written here for you. When I was your age, I often felt afraid and confused. I seldom asked questions and sometimes everyone else seemed to understand things that baffled me. Sometimes I feared school and sometimes I was afraid because my friends didn't include me in activities. I really hated it when my parents got into arguments. I had stomach aches all the time because of these fears.

I wrote this book because I want to help young girls handle the feelings that troubled me when I was young. If you have the same kind of problems I had when I was in elementary school, I think you will feel better if you read one of these meditations each day before you go to school. If you want to, you can share a meditation with your mom or dad or your teacher. They want to know what you're thinking about. Talking over your thoughts with another person is very good for both you and the person you talk to. Try it today and see.

Remember, nobody has to handle her problems all by herself. If there isn't an adult close by, there is another solution. Close your eyes and imagine your guardian angel. She will never leave your side, no matter where you are. I promise you this, but you'll have to find her by yourself. Perhaps you can find her today.

Your friend forever,
Karen Casey

P.S. If you want to write to me, I would love to hear from you. Please write me at Holy Cow! Press, P.O. Box 3170, Duluth, MN 55803.

JANUARY

LEARNING MAY BE THE BEST PART OF GROWING UP.

At school this year, I will learn things I never could have imagined. So will you! We'll learn to read some really hard words. We'll be able to do math problems that were way too hard for us last year. We'll learn about famous people in history. Last year we learned about some of the Presidents. We'll also learn what it means to be a really good friend. According to my dad, this is something we'll learn more about every year of our lives.

Learning to be a good friend is one of the most important lessons because we always need friends. If we have friends, we never have to be lonely. Friends can listen to us when we need to share a secret. Friends can help us get better at softball or math. Learning what it means to be a good friend makes everything else we have to learn a little bit easier.

I will practice learning to be a really good friend today.

BEING GENEROUS IS AN EXPRESSION OF LOVE.

Generosity can be fun. I didn't always think so, though. I feared that sharing a favorite possession meant losing it. One time, I let Jessica borrow my favorite CD to play for her sister, and her sister lost it. The worst part of this was that her sister refused to replace it.

My best friend and I just started sharing part of our lunch every day. It has almost become a game to guess which part she may want. My mom recently suggested that everyone in our family choose three things from our closet to share with another family. Then we took them to the homeless shelter. Actually, I chose my favorite sweater to give away. At first I hesitated, then it felt right. Every time I think about it now, I imagine another little girl loving it as much as I do, and the thought makes me happy.

I can see that every gesture of generosity
makes the world a better place.

WE WILL NEVER HEAR ANYONE ELSE'S THOUGHTS
IF WE ARE ONLY LISTENING TO OUR OWN.
–CATHY STONE

My teacher sometimes accuses me of daydreaming. What does she mean? Probably she means she can tell I'm not really listening to her because I'm staring out the window at a dump truck going by while she is explaining how to do a new kind of math problem. Having my mind someplace other than on what someone is saying to me is an example of daydreaming. Even moms and dads do it! The problem is that I miss the thought the other person is sharing with me.

Every day each of us has specific jobs to do. Maybe it's pouring the juice for breakfast or bringing in the newspaper. I wish the carrier would do his job better and quit throwing the paper in the bushes. One job each of us can do really well every day is to listen to what others are saying. That may be the most important job we have all day.

I will keep my eyes on whoever is talking
and my ears open too! I will be a good listener.

DEVELOPING GOOD HABITS CAN BE A FULL-TIME JOB.

I do have some very good habits. My grandmother Sara recently helped me see what many of them are. While I recalled them, she wrote them on a fancy piece of paper and taped them on her refrigerator. She said that seeing them often keeps them fresh in our minds too. Because I open her refrigerator door dozens of times a day when I stay at her house, I get lots of reminders!

At the top of my list is remembering to say *thank you*. She said not everyone does this as well as I do. I was surprised to hear that. I also am a very good listener. I think I learned this from my dad. He never interrupts me, even when I am telling a long story. I also make my bed nearly every day without a reminder, and I am very careful with my school clothes. I am not sure how I learned that habit. Not from my older sister, that's for sure!

I've learned that expressing a good habit strengthens it.

LIFE ISN'T ALWAYS FAIR.

Are you ever ignored by your friends? It doesn't seem fair, does it? Maybe they all went to the neighborhood ball diamond and didn't ask you, but probably each one thought someone else was going to invite you. They probably didn't realize that no one had until they were on their way home.

A lot of things can happen in a day that seem unfair. Recently my aunt got sick and had to cancel taking me and Amanda shopping. She couldn't help it, but Amanda and I had done extra chores to earn money to spend, and we were bummed out. Even worse things happen sometimes. Dad can't always make it to my ball game because his boss needs him to work late occasionally. That doesn't seem fair, but it can't be helped.

If something happens today that doesn't feel fair, I will remember that life just happens that way sometimes.

IMAGINATION IS MIND POWER.

Pretending I am Superwoman or a Ninja Turtle or even a big sister or the teacher is one of the ways I like to play. My dad says when he was little he often pretended he was a gardener like his neighbor. Now he works in our yard every weekend. My mom thinks we have the best lawn in our neighborhood.

Imagination can help a person quite a bit, according to my parents. I think they are right. Imagination can change whatever is in my mind. I can become brave when I actually feel scared. I can act strong when I feel weak. And best of all, I can act confident when I feel nervous. This is one of the ways I use my imagination regularly.

My imagination can help me out a lot today.

KNOW WHEN AND HOW TO HELP OTHERS.

What do you do when a friend wants to copy your answers on a reading test? I don't want my friend to be mad, but my teacher always says, "Cover your answers." I've thought about why she says to cover my answers. It's because whenever I do someone else's work for them, they aren't learning what they need to know. They'll suffer in the next grade if I help them too much now.

Wanting to help others is a good quality. I just have to be choosy about who and when to help. For instance, I can go to my friend's house after school and practice reading with her. That's a good time to help.

I will offer to help my best friend with something today, but not if it's something she needs to do herself.

FORGIVING OTHERS WHEN THEY HAVE DONE SOMETHING MEAN ISN'T EASY.

Sometimes I get so mad that I just want to scream. Maybe a friend calls me a dirty name behind my back. Or worse, maybe she makes up a story about me that is not one bit true, but everyone believes it, and everyone is laughing at me! So I promise I will stay mad at her forever. The problem with being mad forever is that forever never ends. And even though she was wrong in what she did, I miss hanging out with her. This is a real dilemma.

What can I do when something like this happens? I can talk my feelings over with my mom or my grandmother. Grandma always has a good suggestion for me. She believes that staying mad causes me more harm than my friend did. She suggests I try to see the situation differently. That isn't easy, but it is better than staying mad forever.

If I get mad at someone today, I will try
to look at the situation differently.

Fear is a common feeling.

What are you most afraid of? Teri is really afraid of spiders. They don't scare me, though. My mother is afraid of snakes. They kind of scare me, but my dad says most snakes are harmless. My grandmother says she gets a little bit afraid when strangers come to her door. She always looks through the peephole before she opens the door. I am afraid when I hear my parents fight. I wonder if they'll get divorced like Jenny's parents.

Feeling afraid is normal, but I don't have to stay that way. My teacher says we can learn to watch where we walk and avoid snakes and spiders. We can refuse to let strangers into our houses. We can tell Mom and Dad how we feel about their fights. I guess there are lots of things we can do to stop being afraid.

I am probably going to be afraid at least once today.
I will talk it over with someone.

LOVE IS ALL AROUND IF ONLY I LOOK FOR IT.

Sometimes I think receiving gifts for my birthday and other holidays is the most important sign of love from my family. Everybody likes gifts, but there are lots of other signs of love surrounding us throughout the day. And sometimes absolute signs of love don't actually look that way.

For instance, when Mom told me I couldn't go to Rachael's house after school, that sure didn't seem like love, but there was a reason she said no. Rachael's older sister has been in a lot of trouble with the police because of shoplifting, so Mom doesn't want me around her. Mom is protecting me, and that's certainly love. Having to go to bed by a certain time and eating breakfast before leaving for school are also signs of love. Moms and dads want us to be healthy, and that's a kind of love. Love is often more than a gift in a box.

I will notice and appreciate all the signs of
love that my family shows me today.

DO YOU WAKE UP FILLED WITH WONDER?

I love to look up at the stars at night and wonder how many there are. When we're at Grandma's house, we see even more stars. Dad says it's because there are no city lights out where she lives to outshine the stars. I saw a scientist on television who said there are more stars in our universe than grains of sand on all the beaches in the world. That's a lot of stars!

I love lying on the ground and looking at all the blades of grass in one tiny space and then watching ants crawl through those blades too. Don't you wonder if ants think about what they're doing? There's so much to think about. We're so lucky to be able to think. It means there's always something to do. Even when all of my friends are somewhere else, I can still be busy with my thoughts.

If I am by myself today, I'll remember that I'm not ever really by myself. There are birds and flowers and leaves and rocks to think about. I live in a wonderful world!

ENCOURAGEMENT HELPS ME MOVE AHEAD.

Almost every time I've tried to do something for the first time, like ride my two-wheeler, I was sure I couldn't do it right. I was lucky that someone could help me. My mom was at work, so the man next door hung onto the seat while I tried to ride down the sidewalk. It worked! One of the main reasons was that he told me, over and over, that I could do it. He was right. After that, all I needed was lots of practice.

I can encourage my friends, just like I've been encouraged, when they're trying something for the first time. I don't have to be a grownup to encourage others. All I need to do is tell them again and again that I know they can do it. Pretty soon they'll believe it too!

I will encourage a friend today. It will help me to help her.

OUR OWN GENTLENESS IS A
POWERFUL FORCE IN OUR LIVES.
–PATRICIA HOOLIHAN

I can easily recognize gentleness in others. For instance, when my grandfather offers to take a walk with me, I know he's wanting to share a gentle story. He has lots of them from when he was a boy growing up on a farm. And when my dad suggests that he and I go out for dinner alone, I know I'm needing *special* attention. I am glad he's gentle when he lectures me.

The easiest way for me to express gentleness is toward my cat Sophia. She is very soft and extremely quiet. She is also pretty old. I have had her since I was a tiny girl and she was a tiny kitten. When I am gentle toward Sophia or my mom or even my brother, who is always getting into my stuff, I feel good inside. Grandmother says practicing gentleness makes each person a better person.

Being gentle can help me in many ways today.

NO ONE CAN BECOME A WINNER
WITHOUT LOSING MANY, MANY TIMES.
–MARIE LINDQUIST

Do you hate to make mistakes? I guess most people
do. But I heard in school last week that Thomas Edison,
the man who invented the light bulb, failed more than
500 times while he was trying to make the first light
bulb. I guess he mustn't have hated failure too much.

Failing at something just means I need to try again,
my teacher says. It's no big deal. Even she has to do
lots of things a second time, like when she tried to
draw a picture the class needed to copy for the front
of our reading folders. She had to erase it and start over
three times yesterday. We all laughed. She did too.

*If I make a mistake in anything today, I will
remember I am just like everyone else. Mistakes
can teach me how to be better next time.*

LET YOUR TEARS COME. LET THEM WATER YOUR SOUL.
–EILEEN MAYHEW

Do you ever cry when you don't understand something that's happening? I do. And I cry when I get punished for hitting my sister. Getting punished hurts my feelings. Mother cries when my stepsister doesn't come home at night. Last night, she and my stepdad were both up all night worrying. My little brother cries a lot, but that's what babies do.

My grandmother says tears can wash away sad memories sometimes. Maybe that's a good reason to cry. Grandma cries when she remembers my grandfather. He died last year. I miss him too. He always teased me and made me laugh.

Everybody cries sometimes, and that can be good.
If I cry today, I won't be embarrassed. I will think
of my tears watering the flowers in my soul.

YOU MUST DO THE THING YOU
THINK YOU CANNOT DO.
–ELEANOR ROOSEVELT

The swimming coach at the YWCA recently asked our team to swim from one end of the pool to the other, underwater! I knew I could go from one side to the other. I had done that a zillion times. But from one end to the other seemed impossible. We all groaned, me the loudest. She said we had to be able to do it by the end of the class, so we had better start practicing. At first, Sandra and I both refused. And then Sandra gave in. I was the only one sitting on the sidelines. It was embarrassing.

Finally I jumped in and dove underwater, thinking all the while that I'd make it only halfway to the other end before my lungs gave out. Guess what? My fingers touched the end of the pool while I was still thinking I was in the middle! I had made it! Ms. Henry, the coach, said she wished she had a camera to catch the surprised look on my face.

I can do a lot of things that at first I thought were too hard.

Do you ask for help when you need it?

It's okay to ask someone to braid your hair or help you make the bed. When you want your bedroom or your hair to look extra neat, getting help is good. I ask my teacher to help me understand science experiments too. The more I learn at school, the better my life will be. Nobody knows everything, and everybody needs help with some things.

If your mom has a job, that means she's earning money for working. When she comes home from work, she may ask you to help her by setting the table for dinner. Maybe the neighbor needs help raking his leaves, now that he uses a walker. Someone learning to ride a bike may need help to balance while pedaling. People are all the same—we all need help with something. So we can all feel good by helping someone else too.

I will help a friend at school today, and
I'll ask for help when I need it too.

EXPRESSING GRATITUDE IMPROVES ONE'S OUTLOOK.
–SUSAN EBAUGH

Walking down the street gives me a lot of things to be grateful for. I'm glad to have a safe, uncluttered street to walk on and that I'm not living in a bombed-out city. I'm glad I can walk, that my legs hold me up and move me forward and backward. I know someone in a wheelchair, and she's glad she can go out for a *walk* in her chair. I've learned there's more than one way to walk since Jenna and I became friends.

I feel good about being able to see. And that I have a few friends who like to be with me. And that I have clothes to wear. And that every night I sit down to a good dinner. Not every kid does.

All sorts of things make me happy and grateful. I will look for even one small thing to be happy about today.

ADMITTING I'M WRONG CAN DEVELOP MY CHARACTER.

Nobody likes to admit being wrong. Mom and Dad don't like to be wrong. My teacher doesn't, either. But all of us are wrong part of the time. Maybe I miss a word on the spelling test or forget to make my bed after promising to. It's good to learn that being wrong isn't such a big deal. But it *is* a big deal to be able to admit when *you're* wrong.

It's better not to wait too long after realizing you've made a mistake. Admitting you're wrong right away is much easier than waiting a day or two.

I will probably do something wrong today. I'll try to remind myself that everyone makes mistakes. Being wrong doesn't make me a bad person–it just makes me human.

NEEDING HELP IS OKAY.

Most of us need help with stuff every day. It can start with getting dressed in the morning. Maybe the zipper on my skirt is broken. Maybe I need help pouring milk from the gallon jug. What a mess my little sister made when she dropped it on the floor. Milk even went under the stove!

Mrs. Carl says asking for help with math is better than trying to copy off somebody else's paper. I know that's right. When I looked on Sheila's paper last week, I got the answer wrong, Sheila did too, and we both got in trouble. Next time, I'll ask for help instead.

Asking for help is the right thing to do. If I am unsure about something today, I will ask Mom or Mrs. Carl.

MISTAKES HAPPEN.

Nobody is perfect! Even Katy, my best friend and the smartest girl in my room at school, isn't perfect. She left her permission slip for going on the field trip at home and had to stay at school. She missed an exciting trip to the history museum.

Making mistakes is normal. Adults make them all the time too. Just ask my dad. Mistakes can be big or little. Forgetting to turn the stove off when a pan is on it can be a big mistake. That's one my dad can tell you about. Knocking over a vase can be a big or little mistake, depending on what spills. My little sister knows about that one first hand. Forgetting to bring homework to school can be a *big* mistake, especially if a project is due.

Mistakes can be forgiven and forgotten if I'm willing to accept responsibility for them and try harder the next time.

I will pay close attention to what I am doing.
That can help me avoid mistakes.

WHAT ARE SOME WAYS OF EXPRESSING LOVE?

There are lots of small ways we can tell other people we love them. Words aren't always necessary. Bringing home a pretty rock for Dad to use as a paperweight or carrying a bag of groceries into the house for Mom are ways of saying "I love you" without words. Being really good when company comes to our house, particularly if they are friends from Mom's work, shows her I love her too.

Thanking my family for my home, the food I have to eat, and all of my friends are important ways to express my love, too.

I can begin today by showing Mom I love her. I'll give her a big hug as soon as I finish breakfast, and I'll start my day with an expression of love.

TELLING THE TRUTH IS HARDER THAN IT SOUNDS.

Sometimes I pretend I'm telling the truth when I'm really not. For instance, if I break a brand-new toy, one that cost a lot of money, I've sometimes said I didn't know how it got broken. Or if I forgot to come right home after school, I've pretended that I lost a book or a jacket and had to go find it.

Probably everybody tells a lie once in a while. According to my dad, even adults lie. But it isn't good to do it. Why? Because afterward I feel yucky inside and worry about the truth coming out. Telling the truth, even when I've made a big mistake, doesn't hurt as bad as telling a lie. I learned this the hard way!

I will stop myself today if I am about to tell a lie.
I'd rather feel good inside.

BLAMING SOMEONE ELSE FOR A SITUATION YOU DON'T LIKE IS TOO EASY.

I am too quick to blame others, according to my step-father. One night, I left my bike outside and a neighbor kid borrowed it without asking. I couldn't find it in time for school the next day and had to walk, which made me late, which meant I had to stay after school for being late, which meant I had some explaining to do at dinnertime. I kept insisting that it was actually Timothy's fault because he had moved my bike. My stepdad said, "No way!" If the bike had been in the garage where it belonged, this wouldn't have happened.

Blaming others becomes a habit, I think. My stepfather says it's not easy, but it's so much more peaceful to simply take responsibility for our mistakes. When we quit blaming others, he says, we're mature. I do want to show him I'm maturing. I never hear him blame anyone.

I can be mature today if I am not afraid to take responsibility for all of my actions.

CAN I BE TRUSTED?

If I tell a secret about my family to Kaitlin and ask her not to tell anyone, and then I learn she has told the secret to Megan, the biggest gossip in our school, I have learned the hard way that I can't trust Kaitlin. Being able to trust my friends is very important. Having them know they can trust me too is just as important.

I have been untrustworthy a few times, and I don't feel very good about it. For example, just last week Mother sent me to the grocery for bread and milk she forgot on her way home from work. I bought a candy bar too, and ate it before I got home. She asked me where the rest of the change was, and I said I must have dropped it on the walk home. She gave me a funny look, and I felt pretty uncomfortable. Even a little lie interferes with how I feel about myself.

I want to be trusted, and I want to be able to trust others. Today will give me many chances for both.

THINKING BEFORE ACTING SAVES TROUBLE AND TIME.

Does your mother ever say, "Don't be so impulsive?" Do you know what she means by impulsive? She means reacting to a situation before thinking about what to do. If you act in a hurried way before thinking it through, you may make a big mistake. For example, after my dog got loose and ran through the mud, it wasn't a good idea for me to call him inside. He tracked mud all over the carpet. It's a good thing I grabbed him before he jumped up on the couch, but Mom got mad anyway. Lots of times I end up wishing I hadn't done something after it's too late.

Thinking first is something I can learn to do. For instance, if the new girl at school asks me to play a trick on my friend, I can take the time to think first about how it will make my friend feel. If I'm impulsive instead, I'm going to hurt my friend's feelings.

I will think before I do things today.
Maybe I can save myself some trouble.

FEELING LEFT OUT IS NO FUN.

When my friends get together to do something, I hate getting left out. Don't you? Once in a while all the kids on my block go down to the park and nobody remembers to ask me. I always wonder if they just forgot or if they didn't ask me on purpose. David, my stepdad, says kids sometimes don't notice when somebody's missing from the group. It hurts anyway. It's no fun being left out.

I know sometimes I forget to include someone when I invite kids to come over to my house, but I don't do it on purpose. Mom says we don't have room around the table for everyone. But they probably feel hurt anyway, just like I do.

If I am left out today, I will remember it doesn't mean I'm not liked. There isn't always room for everyone.

WHAT IS SPIRIT?

Spirit is the part of me that feels safe and joyful. It's the part of me that wants to be kind to others. Spirit helps me listen when my teacher or some other grownup is talking. It helps me be polite to a neighbor who hasn't always been so pleasant.

Someone, I think it may have been my grandfather, told me that my guardian angel and my Spirit are the same thing. But even if they aren't, I know they are both with me every minute of the day. I don't have to worry about school, or if my best friend Jamie still likes me, or if my mother is mad at me. My Spirit will protect me and comfort me all day today.

My Spirit is just like my best friend.
All I have to remember is that.

How we treat others is like a boomerang.

My cousin Justin says that how we treat other people comes back to us like a boomerang. For example, if I am really kind to him, he will be really kind back. If I am polite to my teacher, she treats me politely, too. If I am nasty to my older brother, he usually gets mad and chases me. Remembering the boomerang idea saves me a lot of trouble.

The good part about the boomerang idea is that I know what I'll get back from people by how I treat them first. If I'm nice to other people in my life, pretty, happy experiences can happen. I'm going to practice first on my older sister by French-braiding her hair.

I get back from others what I give, so I'm going to be kind, respectful and considerate.

CHOICES ARE NOT IRREVOCABLE.
THEY CAN BE REMADE.
–JULIE RIEBE

What are you going to do today? If it's a weekday, I'll bet you're going to be in school. But you still get to make lots of choices. For instance, who are you going to sit with at lunch? Are you going to ask the new girl to join you and Lauren? Which book are you going to read during free time? When your teacher says to draw whatever you want that begins with a "w," what will you choose?

I never used to think about how many choices I had to make in a day. My dad says that's something that never changes. Choices keep coming at us. Some are hard to make too. For instance, how should I act when someone treats me mean, and what should I do when two friends move away in the same week? It's a good thing I can talk over my choices with Dad or Lauren.

*I will ask for help today if I am
not sure what choice to make.*

WE DO NOT ALWAYS LIKE WHAT IS
GOOD FOR US IN THIS WORLD.
–ELEANOR ROOSEVELT

One day last year, Mother wore her bedroom slippers to her new job. She forgot she had them on! The people in her office laughed and laughed. She said the experience was good for her because it helped her make friends with some of the other women in the office.

A number of things can happen to me that I don't like at the time, but they may be good for me in the long run. For instance, I forgot my homework one day last week. So I had to do it over. This turned out to be good because I had misunderstood the directions. What I had done at home was wrong.

*I will try to remember that I won't like
many things that happen in my life, but that
I can still look for the good in them.*

FEBRUARY

SHARING WITH OTHERS IS A GOOD WAY TO HONOR THEM.

There are so many ways to share with other people. Can you think of some? How about giving half of your candy bar to a friend? Or maybe helping Reshma study her spelling? Aren't those good ways to share your friendship? Maybe inviting the new girl over from down the street to play with your dollhouse is the best way to share today.

Sharing whatever I have with another person makes me feel really good. You probably know someone at school who is really selfish and doesn't like to share. Does she seem very happy? Sharing changes people. Maybe you can share something with a selfish person today. It may make her want to try sharing, too.

Today is a good day for me to share.

IF WHAT WE ARE DOING WITH OUR ANGER
IS NOT ACHIEVING THE DESIRED RESULTS, IT
WOULD SEEM LOGICAL TO TRY SOMETHING ELSE.
–HARRIET LERNER

Is there one thing that makes you really angry? When my brother turns off the light while I'm in the basement, I get really angry. I'm afraid of the dark. My imagination gets the best of me, according to Mom. After he did this for the tenth time last week, I went wild in his bedroom and threw his favorite cars and trucks against the wall. He got the idea. Mom set us both down for a family meeting. She said anger was a natural feeling and she feels it too sometimes, but handling it in more constructive ways was a sign of growing up. She asked us to think of some.

I remembered a book Grandmother once read to us. It told about a girl who planted a flower in her backyard every time she got really mad at someone. By the end of the book, she had a beautiful garden.

Being mad is okay. Handling it without
hurting someone else is my goal.

PRACTICE INCREASES A PERSON'S SKILL.

My friend Trisha is really good at dodging the ball when we play tag at recess. It almost seems like she has eyes in the back of her head because even when the ball is thrown by someone behind her, she moves just in time.

Eddie is really good in spelling. He has won every spelling bee in our class this year. Jacob is just as good in math as Eddie is in spelling. He is always still standing when the members of both teams have missed their answers on a flash card.

I don't think I am the best at anything, but Mom says we all have talent at something. I wonder what mine is?

I will work hard at everything today. Maybe I will see that I am better than I thought at something.

WHAT A STRANGE PATTERN THE
SHUTTLE OF LIFE CAN WEAVE.
–FRANCES MARION

My dad says that bad luck is better than no luck at all, but he's joking when he says that. What is bad luck, anyway? Mom says it might be when it rains during a picnic. When Robyn won the best prize, the ticket to the circus, at my birthday party, we all yelled, "Lucky duck!" But it was bad luck for the rest of us.

Is it bad luck to miss the school bus? Maybe not if the bus slid in the rain. When things happen that we don't want to have happen, we generally say, "Bad luck." But maybe it's good luck instead. Mother says that whatever happens is really what is supposed to happen. If that's right, can there be such a thing as bad luck?

Whatever happens today is what I need,
or so my mother says. I will look for the good
luck hiding behind what looks like bad luck.

CHANGING MY MIND IS OKAY, BUT IT'S IMPORTANT TO DO IT CAREFULLY.

When my friend Holly decided to go home instead of coming home with me after school, I got mad. My feelings were hurt. When people change their minds it affects us, doesn't it? When I'm about to change my mind, it's good to remember that someone else may be hurt by the change too.

It isn't wrong to change my mind. It wasn't wrong when my friend changed her mind and decided to play with someone else. But everyone should think about how others will feel before changing things.

I will stop to think about how my friends will feel if I decide to change my mind about playing with them after school.

PRAYING IS AS IMPORTANT AS EATING BREAKFAST.

When I am scared about the test we are having at school or about going on a field trip, I say a prayer. Mother says that God always hears our prayers. I sometimes wonder how God has time to hear the prayers of so many people. Maybe not everybody prays, but in my family, everybody does. That means God has to listen to at least nine people every day!

When I talk to God, no matter what about, it makes me feel better. I don't feel so alone, and I feel like I can handle what I need to do. Isn't it wonderful having a friend like God, who never gets tired of listening, who is always there to help or comfort me?

I will remember to talk to God
when I need help or reassurance.

I WILL BE THERE AS YOUR SOUNDING
BOARD WHENEVER YOU NEED ME.
–SANDRA LAMBERSON

If you fall down and scrape your knee, making it bleed, you want someone to take a look at it, don't you? If you get an F on a project you did for science class, you want someone to console you and help you understand that you can get better than an F next time. If you're full of fear about a party you've been invited to, you want a grownup to talk to you about being brave. Everybody feels better when others show they're concerned. It means they care about us.

It's just as important to show others I care about them too. If one of my friends falls off her bike or gets the flu and has to miss school, I know it's nice to stop by her house to see how she is. Making an effort to be really kind and considerate to others is always good.

I will practice being especially kind toward others today.

OFTEN GOD SHUTS A DOOR IN OUR FACE,
AND THEN SUBSEQUENTLY OPENS THE
DOOR THROUGH WHICH WE NEED TO GO.
–CATHERINE MARSHALL

Sometimes I ask God for help with a certain problem, but the problem still doesn't go away. I wonder why grownups tell me to ask God for help? When I asked Mom, she told me that God does answer our prayers every time. They just aren't answered until the time is right. She says there's always a right time for every problem to be solved.

Last week I really needed help from God because I was afraid to go to my first gymnastics class. I wanted to stay home, but Mom said I had to go because she had already paid the money. That time I was lucky, and God helped me right away. I walked in the gym and saw Bridget, a friend from second grade. I wasn't afraid anymore.

God will always help me. It just may not be right away.

PEOPLE RARELY FEEL GOOD ABOUT
THEMSELVES FOR BEING UNKIND TO OTHERS.
—MILDRED NEWMAN

I just don't stop to think before I act sometimes. Yesterday my little brother used one of my coloring books, and I really yelled at him and made him cry. I was sorry afterward because he's so young. I wish I had thought first before getting mad. I didn't color so well when I was his age either.

When Mother told me I couldn't go to the park with Emily, I was really awful. I threw my jacket and stomped out of the kitchen. She never even yelled at me, but I felt bad anyway. I knew I was wrong. I wouldn't have done it if I had thought about it first. I get myself in trouble way too often just because I don't take time to think through my actions. Will I ever learn?

Mother says I can grow up a little every day.
I will work on thinking before acting.

TAKING RESPONSIBILITY FOR BEHAVIOR IS A SURE SIGN OF GROWING UP.

Admitting when I've done something wrong, no matter how slight, is a good habit to develop. For example, I spilled orange juice all over the kitchen floor while pouring from a really full carton. I cleaned it up a little bit, but I knew it would be sticky to bare feet. When Mom asked what had happened, I was very, very slow to admit my carelessness. It wasn't a big deal, but I didn't feel very good about holding back the truth for a time.

Another time I was a bit slow to admit I intentionally left the newspaper under the bushes during a rainstorm. I had time to get it before the rain started, but I was mad at Mom for not letting me go to Emma's house, so I "paid her back," if you know what I mean. When the rain stopped and Mom got the paper, she could tell by how I acted what I had done. She didn't say anything, but she didn't need to. I still have some growing up to do, I think.

I will try to be really responsible in all my actions today.

IMAGINATION IS MY FRIEND.

Do you ever pretend you are already grown up? I do. Sometimes I pretend I am a teacher, and I line my stuffed animals up in the bedroom and pretend we are having a math lesson. Last week I pretended I was a doctor and that my brown bear was a very sick little girl, and then I made her well. Last week I secretly pretended that my mom didn't drink anymore. That dream felt really good.

My teacher says it's good to make up dreams. She says it can help in lots of ways. For instance, if I'm afraid of reading out loud, I can practice at home, pretending I am sitting in the circle at school. She says that when we see ourselves doing something, even just in our minds, it helps us when the real experience comes along.

I will use my imagination today to help me.

BE WILLING TO GIVE IN.

Trying to make my twin brother Jake or my friend Samantha play cards my way isn't easy. Everyone has their own rules, and they don't agree with mine. No matter how hard I try to convince Jake or Samantha, they won't give in. That means we're stuck unless I give in. Does that seem fair to you?

It's hard to give in when I think I'm right about something. But I guess I can do it. My foster mother says it's good practice to give in, at least once in a while. She says I'll understand this when I get older. She says if we try it a few times, we'll see it's not such a big thing after all. I'm not so sure. But it's worth a try.

Maybe if I give in rather than keep an argument going, I can have more fun today.

HOPE MAKES US BELIEVE IN POSSIBILITIES.

I hope for lots of things. Sometimes I get lost in my thoughts because I'm hoping for so many things. How about you? Do you ever hope your best friend asks you to sleep over? Do you hope you get a new bike for your birthday? Do you hope you will grow up to be as smart as your older sister? I do. Have you ever hoped your parents would never get divorced? I hoped that many times, but it didn't help.

Sometimes even small hopes count. Maybe you hope for chocolate milk for dinner, or that you don't have to take a bath tonight. Hoping is something we all do. Our grandparents hope for our safety. Our parents hope they have enough money to buy the clothes we need for school. Our brothers and sisters hope we will leave their things alone. Hope gives us something to do when we are afraid of what might happen.

I will hope for good things to happen
to me and all my friends today.

HAVING FRIENDS REQUIRES EFFORT.
–PHYLLIS KIRK

If I'm not nice to the boys and girls in my room at school, I may end up with no friends. I don't want to be alone and have no one to play tag with at recess or to eat my lunch with in the cafeteria. Thomas hardly ever has anyone to talk to. I think it may be because he's so mean to other kids.

To keep friends, I need to be honest, kind, and not argue about every little thing. I want to show others I care about them. Maybe I can share my new book with someone today. An even better idea may be to help Jennifer, the new girl in our class. She isn't a very good reader.

Today I'll talk to Dad about some ways to show I want to be a friend. Then I'll do at least one of them.

To have one's individuality completely ignored
is like being pushed quite out of life.
–Evelyn Scott

Do you ever show off to get attention? Just last week, I rode my bike really fast down the street without touching the handlebars to show off in front of the new girl who moved in across the street. I know she was watching. Once in a while I wear my very best clothes to school because I want Mrs. Hadley to give me a compliment.

It's okay to want attention. Even grownups like it when people notice them. But there are good ways and bad ways to get attention. Bad ways get people's attention at other people's expense, like by interrupting them or making jokes about them or teasing them.

If I want to get some attention today, that's okay. But I will also balance it by giving attention to those around me.

BLAMING OTHERS DOESN'T MAKE US FEEL BETTER.

When I fell down next to my friend Akeesha, I wanted to blame her for tripping me even though I knew inside my heart that she hadn't touched me. When I can't find my coat or hat and it's time to catch the school bus, I really want to yell, "Who hid my coat!" My foster mother says becoming responsible for my own accidents, lost toys, books, and misplaced clothes is part of growing up.

Not blaming someone else is really hard, but it helps me feel like I'm more grown up. I want my foster parents and the other grownups in my life to notice that I'm growing up. It's okay for little kids to blame others. But I'm not really a little girl anymore.

I will stop my mouth if I start to blame
someone for what happens to me today.

GROWING UP HAPPENS IN MANY WAYS.

Brittany is the tallest girl in my room at school. She almost comes up to the teacher's shoulder. I'm still the shortest one in my whole row. Will I ever grow up? I heard my mom tell my brother to grow up, and he's a lot bigger than me. Maybe "growing up" is not just about being bigger. What else does it mean?

When I asked Dad, he said growing up sometimes means thinking like an older person. For instance, stopping to consider what might go wrong before trying an activity that I've never tried before. He says it can mean not being selfish too, and saying *please* and *thank you* every time I get the chance.

*I think I can be a lot more grown up
today if I really want to be.*

I GET ANXIOUS WHEN I FORGET
THAT GOD IS IN CHARGE.

I can get nervous so easily, and so many things trigger my nervousness. I worry that I will miss my ride to school. I get nervous that the girls in my class will leave me out when they play at recess. I often get nervous while trying to fall asleep at night. Mom says that if I thought about God or my guardian angel every time I felt nervous, I could relax more.

Being nervous occasionally is normal. Staying nervous all of the time isn't healthy. I think I will try what Mom suggested. If I feel even a little bit nervous about any-thing, I will draw a picture of God or my guardian angel in my mind. That's what Mom does. She says it helps. I wonder if other people do this too.

*I will try this as an experiment. I think I have
a very kind and comforting guardian angel.*

FIGHTING IS NEVER THE BEST SOLUTION.

I don't like to fight. I get slightly afraid when the older kids fight on the playground at school. Mom says it's good that I don't want to fight, but what if some mean girl or boy starts to chase me? What should I do then? The first thing to do is run, I guess.

I don't like to be chased unless I'm playing a game. If someone starts to chase me and won't stop even after I ask them to, I guess the thing to do is go talk to the teacher or some other grownup. Some kids like to fight. Maybe it's because they aren't very happy. The kids who like to fight don't have many friends. Have you noticed that?

If I feel like fighting with someone today, I will think first. There's a better solution if I think about it.

DREAMS CAN BE MEANINGFUL FOR OUR FUTURE.

Dreams can be significant. My mom has read many books about dreams. She is most interested in night-time dreams, but she said I need to dream about my goals for life too, during the daylight hours. She explained that when she was a girl, she wanted to be a good athlete, so she practiced running, playing tennis, and even joined the basketball team. She said her hard work coupled with the dream gave her the opportunity for a scholarship to college.

I read the biography of Amelia Earhart, and she dreamed of flying a plane around the world. She didn't make that dream, but she was the first female pilot to fly across the Atlantic. Think how much dreaming it took to make that happen! Trying to make our dreams come true gives us direction, energy, and hope. I bet Amelia Earhart had a lot of fun flying!

*Having a dream can make today
and every day pretty exciting.*

Sadness is natural.

Being sad is a natural thing. Lots of things make me sad. If I don't get invited to Katy's after school I am sad, particularly if I know that Erin and Lora were invited. Did I do something to make Katy mad? If Mom cancels her plan to take me shopping, I feel sad. I've saved up $6.15 from my allowance, and I really want a new book. I've read all the books under my bed already.

When our parakeet flew away, I was sad. I wondered if it would know how to survive outdoors. We had always fed it and given it water. I definitely learned how important it is to keep the front door closed. Mom said maybe it would join another group of birds, just like when a new girl moves into our neighborhood.

If I feel sad today, I will see if I can
figure out why. It's okay to be sad.

You can't push a wave onto the shore
any faster than the ocean brings it in.
–Katherine Mansfield

Making someone else do what we want them to do is
pretty hard. I don't even always want to do what
Mother wants me to do. The teacher is always asking
our class to be quiet and we talk anyway. Making my
dog Sandy bark on command or sit up for his food only
works part of the time. Controlling others isn't easy.

When I try to control someone else, I get mad when
they won't go along. Does that ever happen to you? I
have seen it happen to my mom, too. Boy, does she
get mad when my brother and I rough house right
after she has cleaned the family room.

I will follow my rules today. I know what they are.
I will let others follow their own rules too.

Do you express your appreciation to others?

It makes me really happy when my mom says she loves me. It assures me that everything is okay. But I forget to do the same for her. I get in such a hurry that I can't remember she likes hearing she is loved as much as I do.

I know I don't always show my friends how much I like them, either. For instance, yesterday Beth brought an extra dessert for me in her lunch, but it had raisins in it, so I didn't like it. Before I even thought about what I was saying or doing, I spit out the cookie and said *ick!* I didn't even say thanks for thinking about me. I apologized later, which felt good, and she promised that she wasn't mad. The main thing is that I really love having her for a friend, and I didn't show that. I don't think I will make that kind of blunder again.

My friends are very special to me.
I will show them I care today.

WHEN IT COMES DOWN TO IT,
WE ALL JUST WANT TO BE LOVED.
–JAMIE YELLIN

How many ways do you know to show your dad you love him? Is coming the first time he calls one way? How about pulling weeds around the flowers? Setting the dinner table without being asked, or playing with your little sister or brother so they don't bug him when he is on the phone or fixing dinner? One of the best ways, and it's pretty easy to do, is to listen very carefully every time he talks to you. Giving Dad your full attention is giving him a gift. He's probably saying something you need to know.

You don't have to spend money to show
someone you love them. I will show my love
by being really considerate today.

LEARNING TO BE UNDERSTANDING CAN BE DEVELOPED LIKE A HABIT.

I counted on my brother Tim to help me with my multiplication tables, but he couldn't because he got sick. Now I probably won't get an A on the test. Mom says I have to be *understanding*. She says being understanding means that I should show concern for his sickness rather than think only about myself.

I want others to be understanding of me too. For instance, after I told my friend Heather that I could work on the play we are writing for Scouts, I had to go someplace with my aunt instead. Heather didn't get mad. She was very understanding, and I appreciated that. I really want others to show me understanding, so I'll work on showing it too.

When a plan does not work out today,
I will try to understand all the reasons why.

Everyone in this universe is important.
–Josie Bryant

God needs every one of us! Just because you don't like Boyd, the older boy who lives across the alley, or the crabby woman who clerks at the drug store on the corner, doesn't mean God doesn't love both of them as much as God loves you and me. According to my grandfather, God loves each of us the same amount. God needs every one of us too because we all have specific information we need to teach and learn from each other. This doesn't mean that every single person alive has something to teach you, but people who cross your path each day do.

Maybe you can learn that it's better not to be crabby from the lady who is crabby a lot of the time. You know how others feel when you're crabby by how you feel when she talks to you.

*I can learn things from many people,
even the ones I don't like.*

THE WORLD IS A WHEEL ALWAYS TURNING.
–ANZIA YEZIERSKA

It seems like every year one of my best friends moves away. Last year, three girlfriends moved. That was the worst year so far. I wish nothing had to change, but my stepmom says if nothing changed, I would never grow older, my braces would never come off, and my little sister Hannah would never outgrow getting into my favorite things. Some changes are good, I guess.

My teacher says that without change, flowers would never bloom, trees would never grow new leaves, chickens would never lay fresh eggs, we wouldn't have summer vacation, and I'd have to reread the same books over and over again. I guess change is good, even though I don't always like it.

If something changes today that I hadn't counted on,
I'll remember that something good is about to happen too.

SPREADING JOY AROUND IS GOOD WORK.

You know what's really fun to do? Helping other people have more fun. Sometimes Mom is pretty tired in the morning if my baby sister cried all night. Teasing her a little about something gets her to smile. Maybe I'll give some attention to the dog, or better yet, my little brother or sister. Helping someone else have fun is really important.

There are places I go every day where I can help others have fun. Maybe at recess, or maybe I can crack some jokes at lunch time. Playing tag after getting home from school or surprising Mom with a big hug when she didn't expect it can be fun too.

I will count the ways I can help
someone else have more fun today.

> THE FRAGRANCE ALWAYS REMAINS
> IN THE HAND THAT GIVES THE ROSE.
> –HEDA BEJAR

Some people believe giving something away that you really love is one of the kindest things you can do. One of my grandmother's best friends when she was young was an Indian girl, and her tribe believed this. They called it a *giveaway*. On the occasion of a wedding, gifts were given to every person who came to celebrate the marriage. And on the anniversary of someone's death, that person's family gathers all of the tribe together and gives them gifts to honor the dead person, even though he lives in the Spirit world now.

At my church, they say that whenever we give something away, we get back something even better, maybe not immediately, but soon. Maybe you can discuss this idea over dinner at your house tonight.

I am sure I have something I can share today.

MARCH

YOU DON'T HAVE TO BE BORED.

Do you ever feel like there's nothing you really want to do? You've finished reading *Harriet the Spy* and you can't get another book until you go to school Monday. Your best friend is at her grandmother's, so she can't come over. It's too cold to go bike riding and besides, it's starting to rain. What a bummer! That's how boredom is.

My teacher said I never had to be bored unless I wanted to be. She said I could practice writing the alphabet or work on memorizing the subtraction tables. Mom says I can always straighten up my room if there's nothing else to do. She said that she wrote make-believe stories when she was young. She never, ever got bored then. One of her stories even got published in the *Weekly Reader*.

If I am bored today, I will do something to help my mother.

IT IS GOOD TO BE THANKFUL FOR ALL THAT I HAVE.

Did you have enough to eat yesterday? Some girls didn't. Do you have shoes and socks to put on today? Some girls don't. If you look around yourself right this minute, you'll see many, many reasons for being thankful. Being able to read these words is one reason. Having fingers and arms that can move is another.

You have big and tiny reasons for being thankful. Your mother and father love you—that's big. You have your very own toothbrush—that's tiny. You have a sweater you can wear if it is cold—that's kind of big. You have some toys that belong just to you—that's pretty big too.

Being thankful is pretty easy when I look around.
I will take some time today to be grateful for all that I have.

BE STILL AND LISTEN TO THE STILLNESS WITHIN.
–DARLENE LARSON JENKS

Sometimes there's too much noise in my head. I can't listen when my teacher is saying what to do with our math paper because of all the things I am thinking about. Even worse, I don't hear what my best friend is saying about the party she's planning. Mother says this kind of noise happens to her too. She says it comes from not knowing how to be really still inside. She says if she closes her eyes for a minute, it helps. Noticing her breathing helps too.

I wonder why I have so many thoughts running around in my head? I suppose it's because I am curious. It's good to be curious, my teachers says, but maybe it isn't so good when she wants me to just think about math. Many of my thoughts are silly ones too, not ones that are making me one bit smarter.

Today I will practice getting really quiet inside my mind so that I can hear what people are saying to me.

SPIRIT IS PART OF WHAT WE ARE MADE OF.

My friend Elliot says that the Spirit that lives inside of us makes our skin soft to touch. He figured this out after his grandfather died. He noticed when he touched his grandfather's body at the funeral that his grandfather didn't feel soft anymore.

It's comforting to know that our Spirit is as close as our skin all the time we're alive. At my church we believe our Spirit never dies. It just floats away from our body when the body dies. Our minister says that each Spirit goes to be with God after the body dies, which means we will all be together again someday. I don't miss my grandmother as much when I remember this.

My Spirit will be with me all day today.
It will make me feel soft, and warm, and
part of a much bigger world than I can see.

WE CAN BUILD UPON FOUNDATIONS ANYWHERE
IF THEY ARE WELL AND FIRMLY LAID.
–IVY COMPTON-BURNETT

Everybody has a family. The family acts as our foundation, Ms. Glasser says. It provides our security. Some families are much larger than others. My friend Sara has three brothers and two sisters. She has a big foundation! My foundation is small. There is just my dad, my brother, my grandmother and me. My mother doesn't live with us anymore, but she is still part of my family.

My grandmother says it doesn't really matter how large or small a family is if its members are willing to help one another feel brave during the scary times and secure about being loved. In my family, we are really good at both of these things. Dad tells us he loves us every night when we go to bed. And Grandma says that ninety percent of being brave is telling yourself over and over that you can do whatever you are attempting. She even learned to fly an airplane that way, she said!

My family is very important. I will be supportive of it today.

New friends can make our lives more interesting.

Have you ever been the new girl at school? Maybe you haven't ever moved into a new neighborhood, but lots of girls move around a lot. Sometimes it's because their mom and dad quit living together, and the mom moves to a different house. Or sometimes the dad gets a new job in another town, so the whole family has to move. It isn't easy being the new girl at school or in the neighborhood.

If there's a new girl in the classroom today, why not go up to her and say hi? Tell her your name and ask her to sit next to you at lunch. She'll feel a lot better if she's not alone. And you'll feel good about this too. Every time we make a connection like this with someone else, it gives us a warm, fuzzy feeling inside.

I will say hi to someone new today.

WHAT'S IMPORTANT IN LIFE IS
HOW WE TREAT EACH OTHER.
–HANA IVANHOE

When you tell a friend you will take good care of her bike, are you really careful, or do you drop it when you get off instead of using the kickstand? How about when you borrow Sophie's jump rope? Do you remember to take it back as soon as the game is over, like you said you would?

How do you feel when a friend says she will keep a secret you told her, and then you find out she told everyone at the lunch table, and now they're all looking at you? Being able to trust another person is pretty important. Making certain that someone else can trust you is very important too.

I will do exactly what I said I would do today.
I want to be trusted.

SEEK ONLY PEACE.

Almost every day most moms say at least once, "Give me some peace and quiet, will you?" What does that mean? Usually it means she wants you to let her alone so she can think. Do you ever want to be left alone the same way?

Sometimes my mind is just too busy. I'm thinking about what someone said to me yesterday or where I want to go tomorrow. Maybe I'm worrying about whether Rachael is going to invite me to her birthday party. I get tired when my mind is so busy. Maybe I need to ask for some peace and quiet too.

I will see how it feels to get a little
peace and quiet for myself today.

WE CAN LEARN WHAT TO DO WITH OUR FEARS.

Thunder made me really scared when I was little. I always wanted to crawl into bed with my parents. Maybe it affected you too. If it's really loud, with lots of lightening, even now I sometimes get a little bit afraid, but I don't like to admit it to anyone. I usually snuggle up with one of my teddy bears and try to keep my eyes closed. Sometimes I turn on the bedroom light.

When I first started crossing the busy street by my house or went to the store all by myself, I often felt a tiny bit afraid too. But after doing it a few times, I really felt brave. I learned how to handle many things.

Even adults are afraid once in a while. I've heard my mom talk about her fears to her best friend. Maybe I should talk about my fears with Mom or my friend Caitlin.

If I feel afraid of anything I need to do today,
I'll tell someone and that will help.

GROWING UP MEANS FINDING
BETTER SOLUTIONS TO PROBLEMS.

I sure feel sorry for myself when things don't go my way. Yesterday I was supposed to be the monitor and hand out the papers at school, and my teacher forgot. She asked Kelley instead. I felt sorry for myself for a while, then I talked to my teacher. She let me feed the hamster instead. I was glad I just asked instead of keeping to myself and pouting.

Mom says I need to handle difficult things more gracefully. When I feel sorry for myself, I need to look for a graceful way to take care of my feelings. That may be by talking to my teacher, my mom, or my best friend.

If something doesn't happen my way today,
I will find a graceful way to handle it.

WHAT DOES BEING SUCCESSFUL MEAN?
DOES IT MEAN BEING RICH?

I heard Alex say the new family next door to him is really rich. They have a boat and a giant television. My Aunt Carolyn said her new friend must be rich and successful because she has a very fancy house and a new Corvette. My teacher says you can be successful in lots of different ways and it doesn't necessarily mean having money at all. Mom agrees with her.

Mom says having really good friends is one kind of being rich. She says using and developing our talents is a way to share a rich mind. It's nice to know there are lots of ways to be successful besides money. Maybe I won't ever have extra money, but that doesn't mean I won't be rich and successful in other ways.

I am a success when I have good friends and use my talents.

LAUGHTER HELPS ME FEEL BETTER INSIDE.

My brother makes me laugh a zillion times a day. Sometimes he makes me laugh when I really shouldn't, like when he makes a face behind the baby-sitter's back after she has scolded him. Mostly he does really funny things that make my mom and dad laugh too. Last night he put all of his clothes on backward before coming to the dinner table. He even wore a pair of my dad's shoes, since he couldn't get his own on backward. Mom took his picture when we couldn't stop laughing.

Laughing can make us feel good all over. Don't you wish you could laugh more of the time? Hey, maybe you can. Maybe we all can! There aren't any laws against it! Mainly we have to be willing to laugh.

I can practice laughing just like
I practice my spelling words today.

I AM LEARNING TO ACCEPT
RESPONSIBILITY FOR MY BEHAVIOR.

Everyday I'll probably have to say I'm sorry to someone. If I'm grouchy when I wake up, I may say something mean to a member of my family. They aren't the reason I'm grouchy, so I should say, "I'm sorry." Maybe in my rush to get ready for school, I spill my milk. If so, I should help to clean it up and say, "I'm sorry."

Running into a classmate because I'm not watching where I'm going is another reason for being sorry. Being mean to the person behind me in line in the lunchroom or laughing when someone misses a question the teacher asks are also very good reasons for saying I'm sorry. Whenever I do something I wouldn't want someone else to do to me, it's time to say, "I'm sorry."

☙

If I have hurt someone else, whether accidentally or on purpose, I can begin to make it right by saying and really meaning it, "I'm sorry."

WE ARE ALL DIFFERENT, YET EQUAL.

Did you ever look carefully at everyone in your room at school? No two people look much alike, except for the twins Sam and Max. Many aren't even the same color. Antonio has darker skin than me. Lauren is even darker than Antonio. Emma has the curliest hair. Three kids wear glasses. We really are all different.

Mother says it's good there are so many differences. She says we need to understand that looking one way or another isn't a very big deal. Our differences are important, but they don't make any one of us better or worse than anyone else. We are equal, no matter what our differences are.

*I will remember that I am as good
as all my classmates today. I'll also remember
that I'm no better than the rest of them.
We are all equal, and that's important.*

DO YOU FEEL LUCKY?

I do. I have a school to go to. I have clothes to wear, warm ones when it's chilly, and shorts for the hot days. I have cereal for breakfast and hot lunches at school every day. Some days my mom leaves a treat for me after school too. I have lots of reasons to feel lucky.

Not all kids are as lucky as me. Kirsten comes immediately to mind. Her mother was killed in an accident last year. Some days Kirsten doesn't have on really clean clothes. Probably her dad doesn't have time to get all of the work done. I can't imagine how much I would miss my mom if anything happened to her.

Today I'll try not to take for granted all the ways I'm lucky.

CHANGING YOUR MIND IS A TRICKY THING.

Do you ever tell a friend you will come to a sleep-over and then you don't want to go when that night comes? That time when Alyssa changed her mind, I was really upset. I had counted on her coming. Mom had even rented a video for us to watch. I had spent some allowance money on candy for us too.

When a friend changes her mind about doing some-thing you had counted on, you may feel upset. The same is true when you change your mind. Should you just go ahead and do something that no longer feels right? That's hard to figure out. It's good to discuss questions like this with one of your parents. They know more about changing their minds.

*If I feel like changing my mind about something
I wanted to do last week, I'll ask Mom or Dad to
help me handle it. I don't want to hurt my friend's
feelings, but I need to figure out what feels right to me.*

COOPERATING WITH OTHERS
IS A SIGN WE ARE GROWING UP.

My mother says cooperation is necessary in our family because she has a very hard job at the newspaper, and she works overtime two or three times a week. She needs my sister and I to help get dinner, set the table, do dishes, and do the laundry too. Some days I hate to help. I just want to curl up on my bed and read.

In school last week, Mr. Andrus asked our class to make a list of the ways we had cooperated in the last week. I ended up with more examples than anyone! It made me glad that Mom expects me to help out at home. Mr. Andrus said that learning to cooperate at this age will help us when we grow up. I think I would like to be a dentist like my Uncle Hank. I wonder if he cooperates with others at his clinic?

I will be quick to cooperate if someone needs my help today.

MAKING A NEW FRIEND CAN BE HARD.

Do you ever wish a certain girl would be your friend, but you don't know how to ask her? Did anybody ever ask you to be her friend? Sometimes kids don't really ask, they just start talking to each other. When Jamie and I became friends, she just walked up to me and asked if I wanted to play jacks. I said yes, and we've been friends ever since.

My teacher says it's good to make friends with someone new in our class. It would be pretty lonely to move to a new school where you didn't know anyone. I'm so glad I have a lot of friends.

I will be on the lookout for a new boy or girl today at school. I will offer my friendship.

PROBLEMS TEACH US THINGS.

There are many kinds of problems. There are math problems every day. There are science problems on Friday. There is the problem of who to play with when both Margo and Jamie ask me to come over after school. Even what to eat for lunch can be a problem because some days I like everything the cafeteria has. Sometimes deciding whether to spend the weekend with my dad or my mom is a big problem.

Mom says solving problems of any kind is good practice. She says problems are one thing you can count on having for the rest of your life. When I'm older, I wonder if my problems will get any harder than knowing who to spend the weekend with.

I will have a few problems today, but I can solve them.

COMPARING MYSELF WITH A FRIEND
CAN MAKE ME FEEL INSECURE.

Everyone's good at something. Laurie jumps rope really well. She can even jump a double rope. Bryan can outrun most of the kids on the block. Caitlin can paint really beautiful birds and flowers.

We're all good at some things. When I remember this, I don't feel as bad when I see I can't paint as well as Caitlin or run as fast as Bryan. Bryan probably wishes he could read as well as I do. None of us does the same at everything. That's what makes this an interesting world, my dad says.

I will practice what I do best today.

LET'S NOTICE THE LOVING ACTS OF OTHERS.

My mother told me that love can be expressed in many ways. She said there are as many small ways we can show others we love them as there are colors of crayons to choose from. So I thought about this, and here's what I figured out:

When I pull a clean blouse out of the closet today, it's because somebody lovingly washed it for me. They may have ironed it, too. When I was thirsty, there was milk or juice in the refrigerator because someone loved me enough to go shopping. Mom comes to get me when a friend calls on the phone, and even something that small is a very loving act.

Doing even a small thing can be a sign of my love for somebody today. I'll begin by offering to help Mom.

BEST FRIENDS CAN MAKE THE DAY MORE FUN.

Did somebody choose you as a best friend? Sometimes when I look at my classmates, they all seem to be paired up with a best friend already. That's probably just my imagination, though. Plenty of girls ask me to come over for parties and stuff.

Being a best friend doesn't just happen. It takes work. If I want a best friend, I have to be kind. I have to be willing to share my favorite things. I have to be willing to take turns. If I'm not anybody's best friend right now, maybe I should just enjoy all the good friendships I already have.

I can be kinder to everyone today.
It will make all of my friendships better.

BEING SCARED IS NORMAL.

Everybody is scared part of the time. Even my parents get scared by some things. Maybe riding a roller coaster is too scary for them. A loud thunderstorm may scare me, but not them. It's a good thing everybody isn't scared by the same things because we can help each other feel brave.

Teachers and parents often tell kids to stay away from strangers. They don't mean to scare us, but they want us to be careful. Going to a new classroom or playing with some new kids in the neighborhood may make me feel shy or even a little scared. That's okay. Lots of people, kids and adults, are a little shy when meeting people for the first time. I just have to remember this is how it is, even for Mom and Dad, to feel a little braver.

It's okay for me to be scared of certain things. Nobody is totally brave all the time. That's what I need to remember.

EVERY PERSON IS RESPONSIBLE FOR ALL THE GOOD
WITHIN THE SCOPE OF HER ABILITIES.
–GAIL HAMILTON

Mother says that every single person I come into contact with has a lesson to teach me. I'm sure I know what she means. I can understand that my teacher has lessons for me. But she says that even Cory, the boy next door who is often mean to me, can teach me some lessons too. I guess he shows me how not to treat other people. That may seem like a funny way to teach and learn a lesson, but Mother says we learn in many ways.

It can be fun to see if I can figure out what lesson each person is trying to teach me today. One lesson I can teach everybody else is that I'll look for the good in them and praise it.

I'll be both a teacher and a student today.

IT'S ALWAYS BEST TO THINK BEFORE TAKING ACTION.

It's not so easy to remember to think a minute before yelling at someone who makes me mad. Sometimes I've even hit a friend and then I've felt really sorry or even scared that I've done it. I always end up remembering Mom or Dad or my teacher saying, "Don't speak or act before thinking over what you are about to do." Why is it so hard for me to slow down?

Mrs. Powers, the principal at my school, says she sometimes counts to ten before she answers a person who has made her mad. Counting to ten isn't too hard for anyone who knows how to count—we do it all the time during math period and when we are playing hide-and-go-seek. Now we can practice it in a new way, and this way will help us calm down and do the right thing.

I will practice counting to ten before
I answer anybody who makes me mad today.

WHAT DO WE LIVE FOR, IF IT IS NOT TO MAKE
LIFE LESS DIFFICULT FOR EACH OTHER.
–GEORGE ELIOT (MARIAN EVANS CROSS)

"What have you recently done to help out one of your parents?" This is a question we had to write an answer to in school last week. My mom and dad both have jobs, so my brothers and I have lots of chores at home. I wrote a pretty long list of ways I had helped. The next question asked how we had helped a friend. Just the day before, I had helped Samantha draw a map of the United States. It wasn't really that hard because we could copy it from a book, but I am better at drawing than she is. She shared her dessert with me at lunch that day.

My mom says that anytime we help someone else, we are helping ourselves at the same time. This is how it works: Helping others makes you feel good about who you are. And feeling good about yourself makes it easier for you to be successful when you try a whole new activity. Our confidence grows when we are willing to help others.

I will increase my confidence by helping someone else today.

THE ORDINARY HUMAN BEING THINKS
ABOUT TWELVE THOUSAND THOUGHTS A DAY.
–SUSAN SMITH JONES

Mom has to remind me to slow down and think first before I do stuff. For instance, when I finish breakfast and jump up from the table, accidentally knocking her cup of coffee over, usually I can't even remember what was in my mind at the time. Whatever thought it was, it didn't help me avoid an accident!

My teacher reminds us to think before writing down answers on the science test. Why? If I don't think about the answer first, I might write down the wrong thing. I always have some thought in my mind. During science, my thoughts should be on the question my teacher asked.

Almost everything I do would be done better if I stopped and thought about it first. Even making my bed or getting dressed in the morning could be done better.

Sometimes taking three deep breaths can help me slow down and focus on what I need to do. I will try that today.

DECIDING ON THE RIGHT THING
TO DO ISN'T ALWAYS EASY.

There's always a right thing to do. Like if a friend is mean, should you be mean back? My foster mother says the right thing is to just walk away and find someone else to play with. If a friend wants to copy from your math paper, what's the right thing to do? The teacher says everybody needs to learn how to do the work alone. Maybe you can help your friend later. Letting her copy isn't the right thing because she won't learn anything that way.

I will try to do the right thing today, no matter
what I would rather do. If I need help figuring this out,
then I'll talk it over with Mom, Dad, or Aunt Jane.

WE ALL HAVE UNIQUE STRENGTHS AND TALENTS.

I want to be really good at everything I try. I remember when I first tried ice skating. I kept falling down, and it made me so mad. My best friend Amy never fell. It didn't seem fair. She didn't practice any more than me, but she still never fell, at least while I was watching.

Being good at dodge ball or basketball takes practice too, even though I think I should be able to play as well as the best kid in my class. I'm never going to be an expert at some stuff, though. Even though I study hard, I may never be an expert in math. My dad said math was always his hardest subject too.

Not everyone can play the piano very well, even with lessons. I heard Mom say her aunt wasn't a very good cook. You don't have to be good at everything, I guess. That's a relief!

Today I will notice what I'm good at
and be thankful for those talents.

PEOPLE NEED JOY, QUITE AS MUCH AS CLOTHING.
–MARGARET COLLIER GRAHAM

Sometimes I wake up excited because something really special has been planned for the day. Maybe my class is going on a field trip or my dad is taking me out for dinner all by myself, just the two of us. Or maybe my mom promised that I could wear my new shoes to school. Lots of things make me excited and full of joy.

I can decide to be excited even if nothing really special has been planned. Getting excited is something I can do for no reason at all, perhaps just by looking forward to all the good things that can happen. Each day is lots more fun if I decide to look forward to it.

I will choose to be really happy today.

SOME DAYS WE FEEL HAPPIER THAN OTHER DAYS.

Some people believe you are as happy as you make up your mind to be. My grandmother has this idea. She said she adopted this idea from Abraham Lincoln, a former president. Supposedly he said this more than 100 years ago! I am not so sure I agree with my grandmother. Yesterday I was not one bit happy. My dad cancelled our dinner plans at the last minute, and I couldn't be happy about that! When I mentioned this to her, she said maybe I could find another reason to be happy. For instance, she was willing to play Monopoly with me after we had dinner at home.

My best friend's dog recently got run over. That's not something a person can be happy about either. Again, my grandmother said sadness was perfectly normal. But she said we could always look for something to feel good about even when a bad situation has occurred. The good thing was that my friend didn't run after her dog when it chased the squirrel. If she had, she might have gotten hit by the car too.

I may feel happy and sad today. Whatever I feel is okay.

APRIL

PRAYING FOR OTHERS HELPS US AS WELL AS THEM.

Have you ever heard someone say it's good to pray for whoever you're angry at? That seems kind of silly. When I'm mad at someone, I either want to ignore her or maybe yell at her. Why should I pray for her?

Adults have funny ideas about things but maybe they are smarter because they are older. My dad says praying for someone we're mad at takes away our anger, and then we feel better. I don't always want to feel better when I'm mad.

I think I'll try Dad's idea if I get mad at someone today. Maybe it will help me to do this.

OFTEN WHEN WE'RE BEING
TOUGH AND STRONG, WE'RE SCARED.
–DUDLEY MARTINEAU

Sisters and brothers fight. Moms and dads fight too. Neighbors sometimes fight. Fighting upsets me. When I fight, I end up with a stomach ache. I guess fighting is bad for my health! There are many reasons why people fight. My stepdad thinks people fight because they're scared. I know when I fought with Hannah yesterday, it was because I was scared that she was taking all the cookies.

Fighting sometimes happens because one person wants to be in charge. When Mom and I fight, it's because she wants me to do something I don't want to do. When the neighbors fight a lot, Mom says it's because Mr. Gray stays out too late at night.

If I feel like fighting or arguing today, I'll ask myself why and try to understand why I'm feeling the way I do.

HAVING PROBLEMS IS A SIGN OF BEING ALIVE.

Nobody's free of problems. At least that's what Tiffany's grandmother says. Part of everybody's job is to learn how to solve problems. The problems you have at school are easy compared to the problems adults have to solve. For instance, my dad got fired from his job. Now he has to find a new one—really quickly, Mom says. Lots of people got fired where he works, so they'll all be looking for new jobs.

The only problem I had yesterday was how to sound out some new words in reading. They were hard words, but I managed to figure them out. Making my mind get really quiet is the first thing to do when solving any kind of problem, whether it's a small problem or a big one.

I will solve all my problems today if I get
really quiet first. I will listen for what to do next.

TO SHOW GREAT LOVE FOR GOD AND
OUR NEIGHBOR, WE NEED NOT DO GREAT THINGS.
—MOTHER TERESA

Does it make you feel good when your mother reminds you that she loves you? If you have just done something pretty obnoxious, like stomping out of the kitchen because you didn't like what she made for breakfast, it may surprise you that she loves you. Maybe she even says that she loves you but doesn't love how you are behaving.

Mom is like God in that way. God loves us no matter what we do, according to my Sunday School teacher. God notices all of our efforts toward goodness and accepts our imperfections. If we make a mistake and do something that is not very nice, God won't decide to quit loving us.

❧

God will love me today no matter what I do,
but I will be as good as I can be anyway.

OPINIONS ARE INDIVIDUAL IDEAS.

Do you know what opinions are? They're what you believe about certain things. Like my mom's opinion that *Beavis and Butthead* are too violent. She doesn't want me watching them on television. My dad has an opinion about camping. He thinks it's the best activity families can do together.

My teacher's opinion is that all children should be quiet unless called on to answer questions. That's a hard one for most of us to go along with, especially Brittany. She talks out of turn all of the time. My opinion is that school is pretty fun. I love to learn new words.

Having opinions is part of what makes me an
interesting person. Today I will honor my opinions
by thinking and also talking about them. I will honor
other people's opinions by listening to them.

CHANGE IS AN EVERYDAY EXPERIENCE.

Have you ever had to change schools in the middle of the year? I haven't, but my friend Lisa has already changed twice since December. She says it isn't hard, but I think I'd be scared. What if nobody liked me?

My teacher says we make changes all of the time, but mostly we don't notice them. For instance, she changed our reading group from the morning to the afternoon and I never realized it until it was time to go home. She changed the bulletin board too before we came to school this week and only Stephanie noticed. It's good to remember that everything changes.

Some changes are harder to experience than others.
If I have to make a big change sometime soon,
I'll try to remember that change is a part of
life and so are all the feelings that go with it.

I'M WRONG ALMOST AS OFTEN AS I'M RIGHT.

Nobody's right all the time. The principal at my school may be right more often than us kids, but even she makes mistakes. Sometimes the clerk at the grocery rings up the wrong price, and Mom has to point it out to get the correct change. When Dad ran the stop sign, he was wrong. It's a good thing there were no cars there, or he might have hit somebody. That would have been a very sad wrong.

Being wrong isn't the end of the world. It helps to remember that mistakes don't need to be hidden—they're okay.

I will probably make a mistake today.
I'm not perfect, but I am the best me I can be.

SPORTSMANSHIP CAN BE DEVELOPED.

Are you good at sports? I'm a pretty fast runner. Even though boys can usually run faster than girls, the twin sisters who moved into our school district last year can outrun every boy in our whole school! My mom said their parents are good athletes too.

I'm not good at everything I try. Nobody is. I have worked really hard at shooting baskets, but I still don't get very close to the rim most of the time. Sara has the magic touch: she's always making baskets. The other day I told her she was really good, and her whole face lit up. That made me happy too. It's actually nice when our friends are better at some things than we are. That way we can trade praises for the things each of us is good at.

Being glad for how good others are is good sportsmanship. Are you a good sport around your friends?

I will work on sportsmanship today.
Praising others will be my assignment.

BEING IN CHARGE IS SELDOM FUN FOR LONG.

Bossing my friends around hasn't made me very popular. They probably didn't like it when I insisted they play a game by my rules when they'd rather be doing something else. When a friend starts bossing me around, I don't like it either. Nobody is very happy when someone else tries to take charge. Why do people always want to take charge of others?

My stepmother Betsy says that's how people are. Everybody wants to be in control. It just doesn't work though. Everybody can't be in control. Some of us have to just follow along, or learn to take turns.

I will ask my friend to take turns with me today.
First one of us will take charge and then we'll switch.

I DON'T HAVE TO LIKE EVERYBODY,
BUT I CAN STILL BE CONSIDERATE.

There's a big difference between not liking someone and being mean to them. Just because I don't like the boy who sits behind me at school, or the girl who lives across the street, I don't have to call them names or play mean tricks on them.

What I do when I don't like someone is pay extra attention to the kids I like a lot instead. Sometimes I watch my friends who like the kids I don't like. Mom says I can learn something I need to know that way. My best friend at school actually likes the boy who sits behind me. Maybe I can learn why.

*I may not like everybody I am around today,
but I can be kind and considerate anyway.*

THERE IS BODY PAIN AND HEART PAIN—
THEY BOTH HURT.

There are many kinds of pain. Last week, my mother stubbed her toe on the stove, and did she yell! I went to the dentist to get a cavity filled and after the numbness went away, my jaw hurt. My dad got rear-ended in his car almost six months ago. He's had pain in his neck ever since.

The minister at church says that some pain can't even be seen. That kind can be the worst of all. My grandmother has been in pain ever since my grandfather died. But I can't see what hurts. My mother says it's her heart. She's lonely. I think I'll bring her a flower today.

I will do what I can to ease the pain of someone I love today.

WHEN I AM LONELY, THERE ARE WAYS I CAN REACH OUT.

Do you ever feel lonely? Most people do. I can tell my mother is lonely ever since her boyfriend got transferred to another city. I've heard my grandmother talk many times about being lonely since her neighbor died. It's nice to have companions and friends, isn't it?

I know some things I can do if I'm feeling lonely. I can call the new girl in my room and ask her to come over and play. I can go visit the neighbor who always seems to be in her yard all alone. Sometimes reading a good book helps—it's like the characters are keeping me company. I can ask my mom if I can help her do something around the house. Just getting busy with something makes my loneliness disappear.

I can choose to be lonely today, or I can choose to do something helpful for someone else.

GOOD DEEDS HELP MAKE THE WORLD A BETTER, KINDER PLACE.

Doing a favor for someone who has not even asked for one is a good deed. Maybe I can do a good deed for a neighbor and make her very happy. I can sweep her walks. I can carry the fallen tree limbs from her yard out to the street. If her newspaper goes into the bushes instead of onto her porch, I can get it for her.

Mom and Dad are easy to do good deeds for. Picking up the baby's toys and cleaning up the food the dog spilled around his dish are good deeds. So is making sure I clean up all the messes in my bedroom, the kitchen, and the backyard. Anything I do that Mom or Dad would have to do if I wasn't around counts as a good deed.

I wonder how many good deeds I can do today?

LAUGHING FEELS GOOD.

Having a great big laugh feels really good. It tickles my insides. Does it do that to you? Funny jokes make me laugh. So does watching my dad play a trick on my mom. Last week, just for fun, he hid all the dinner plates and left a note in the cabinet saying the plates and the family were at her favorite restaurant, waiting for her. Sometimes my little brother puts his shoes on the wrong feet. That makes all of us laugh.

When I forget to comb my hair sometimes, I laugh when I look in the mirror. One time I wore one brown shoe and one black shoe to school. That really made me laugh! It's good to be able to laugh at ourselves. Mother says that can be the best time of all to laugh.

I will enjoy all the ways there are to laugh today.

What is a miracle?

When someone wins the lottery, everybody says, "It's a miracle!" Or when my friend Sara got her new bicycle, she thought it was a miracle, especially because her mom and dad had gotten divorced. What about waking up from a bad dream? That seems like a miracle too because the dream seems so real. Are all these things really miracles?

How do I decide what's really a miracle? I can ask my teacher or my mom, but they won't necessarily know. Maybe all that counts is if I'm happy about what's happening in my life. If I think about a miracle as my ability to be happy, then I can have miracles every day.

I will notice all the small and large miracles,
all the moments of happiness, in my life today.

KINDNESS IS A STATE OF MIND.
–THELMA EBAUGH

My grandfather says people can never be too kind. He says the nicest thing I can do for anybody is to treat them as if they're very special to me. Last week, I told Olivia how much I liked her, and she seemed so happy to hear it. I think it stayed in her mind all day because she was smiling every time I looked at her.

It isn't very hard to be kind. Just saying *please* or *thank you* whenever I can is one way of being kind. So is not gossiping about a friend, even when I'm angry at her. There are many small ways to show kindness. I will practice this by being very kind to my mom, my dad, my sister, and the new bus driver.

I wonder if I can do a dozen kind things today?
Mom says if I give kindness, it comes back multiplied!

SHOWING OTHERS WE LOVE THEM IS LIKE GIVING THEM A GIFT.

Even in very small ways I can show my stepmom Stella that I really love her. I can help her by clearing the kitchen table after breakfast. I can pull the covers up on my bed. I can hang up my towel in the bathroom. I can pick up all my games, my books, my crayons, and all my shoes from the middle of the family room.

When I pick up after myself, I save Stella from having to do extra work. That's a good way to show her I love her.

Today I'm going to do at least three small jobs to show my stepmother or somebody else that I love her.

BLAMING IS HOW WE AVOID RESPONSIBILITY.

I always want to blame someone else for my mistakes. Last week, I forgot to turn the water off in the bathroom sink. Water even ran into the living room. At first, I said I didn't do it, that my little sister must have, but Dad knew better. None of us wants to admit when we are wrong. Mom says that it is "human nature" to blame others, but that doesn't mean it's the right thing to do. I must be afraid I'll get yelled at for mistakes because I always think first about blaming someone else.

It isn't honest to blame someone else for what I did, or to claim I knew nothing about it. It isn't fair to the person I blamed. They know I'm lying, and I know it too. We both know I'm pretending I had nothing to do with something I did.

I will be very careful not to blame anyone else today, even though it will mean I'll have to admit I did something wrong.

ALL MY TROUBLE WITH LIVING HAS COME FROM FEAR.
–ANGELA L. WOZNIAK

Nobody is brave all the time, even Dad. I know my mother doesn't like it when it storms really hard after dark. Sometimes she makes us go to the basement in case a tornado is close by. Sometimes I think there's something creeping around my bedroom after Mom has turned out the light. Then I have to get up and check to make sure nothing is there.

Dad says people generally get braver as they get older. He also says it's okay to be scared part of the time, no matter how old you are. Talking to God helps him when he feels afraid, and sometimes that helps me too. Fear is normal.

If I feel afraid today, I will remember that I am not alone.

EVERYBODY GETS LEFT OUT SOMETIME.

Last week Whitney asked everybody in our swimming class except me to come to her pizza party. I felt really sad when she left me out. Mom said maybe she just forgot. I could have asked her if she forgot, but I was scared to. What if she said she just didn't want me to come?

Everybody gets left out once in a while. Mom said the other day her two best friends didn't ask her to go for a walk with them. She felt bad too. Why do we feel such pain if we are left out? Probably we think it means we aren't liked. But then I'd never asked Samantha to sleep over. And I like her. So maybe not getting invited to do something isn't really such a big deal.

If I get left out of something today, I'll try not to get upset.
It doesn't necessarily mean I'm not liked.

I LIKE TO SHOW OTHERS THAT THEY MATTER TO ME.

Sharing a treat that Mom sent in my lunch shows Maia that she's my friend. Asking Jackie to sleep over this weekend is a nice way of telling her she's important to me. Helping Mom clean up the family room and bringing in all the toys from outside shows her I love her.

My teacher says we all need to know that we matter. If we aren't noticed on the playground or chosen to join a dodge ball team, we can forget that we matter. But we do, she says.

Today I'll make sure my friends
know they are important to me.

DYING IS PART OF LIVING.

Dying is really hard to understand. I wonder what actually happens? Does your heart just suddenly stop beating? Sometimes I watch people die in the movies or on television. My grandparents got really sick and died many years ago, but I still see them in my dreams some nights. Dead birds in the street, or even dead cats sometimes make me think of my grandparents. I wonder if their Spirits are all together in one place?

I like to think people go to heaven when they die. I imagine they're all there, having a lot of fun, laughing together, and just waiting for the rest of us. That's a good picture to have in my mind.

I don't have to worry about dying, but it's interesting to think about it and to remember people I've loved who have died.

THERE IS A DIVINE PLAN OF GOOD
AT WORK IN MY LIFE.
–RUTH P. FREEDMAN

Lots of things confuse me. For instance, I'm confused by the new math we're learning in school. I'm confused by why girls in my circle can read better than boys. I'm confused by why Betsy's dad moved away last week. She says he still loves her, but why would he move away? Grownups are confused by lots of things too. I heard my dad say only yesterday he didn't understand why Mr. Brown got another new car when their house needs new windows and a paint job.

Maybe it's not so important to understand everything. Mom says I can always ask her when I'm confused and she'll try to make sense of things for me.

If I am having trouble understanding something,
I will ask an important adult in my life for help.

CRITICISM IS HARD TO LISTEN TO.

When Dad says I haven't cleaned my room very well or my teacher calls me to her desk to talk over mistakes on my math test, I feel pretty uncomfortable. I want praise for everything I do, even though Dad says this isn't realistic. When I'm not praised, my feelings get hurt.

Part of growing up is being able to listen to criticism without getting angry or hurt. I need to remember that part of learning to do something better is first seeing what I've done wrong.

*I don't have to get upset today if I have to
do my homework twice or remake my bed.
It'll help me learn to do everything as well as I can.*

NEEDING HELP IS HUMAN.

I need help a lot. Often I can't read all of the words in the book I get at the library. Sometimes I get books that are too hard for me. Sometimes I need help buttoning my blouse because the buttons are so tiny they're hard to hold onto. If it's completely full, the gallon milk jug is too hard to lift by myself.

Knowing when to ask for help is part of growing up. I can do lots of things alone, but it's smart to ask for help when I really need it. And for sure I'll ask for it in an emergency.

When he has to lift something that's really heavy, my dad asks for help. I'll ask for help when I need it too.

BELIEVING IN OURSELVES
MEANS WE HAVE CONFIDENCE.

How many times a day do you start to say, "I can't do this"? Most kids and even many adults don't believe they can do what is expected of them. I remember when Mr. Gerard, my second grade teacher, put a new kind of math problem on the chalkboard. My first thought was, "Oh, no, I can't do that." But he helped me. And I did learn it.

Putting fear out of mind helps me try new things. I can change my thoughts, and pretty soon, I discover that nothing is too hard for me if I go slow and ask for a little help.

*I will not be afraid to ask Jessica or Mom
to help me do something new, to help me
ignore the voice that says I can't do it.*

DO YOU KNOW WHAT IT MEANS TO HAVE A HEALTHY LIFE-STYLE?

Nobody can always prevent sickness. But everyone can learn how to take better care of herself, according to my Aunt Sandra. She is overweight, and she wishes she had been more careful with what she ate when she was younger. She frequently makes suggestions to my mother about what she should be feeding my sister and me so we don't gain too much weight.

I am not very fond of carrots and broccoli, but I love the dip my aunt makes for them. It's a good way of getting used to them, Mom says. Abbey and I recently enrolled in gymnastics too. I didn't want to go at first, but now I like it. Mom says it's important to be strong and gets even more important as women get older. She goes to a gym every day for a workout. I think I may want to do that when I get older too. She has a lot of energy, which she says comes from exercise.

*I will contribute to my health today by
what I eat and by exercising like my mom.*

I CAN HAVE FUN ALONE.

When I was little, I thought for me to have fun somebody had to play with me or maybe read to me. Now that I'm older, I realize I can have fun all by myself. This is good because there isn't always somebody around to entertain me.

One of the things I like to do when I'm alone is pretend I'm grown up. Some days I put on my mother's lipstick, fingernail polish, and perfume. When I was younger, I even dressed up in her old clothes. I like to write stories too. Now that I've learned to use the dictionary, I don't have to make pictures for the words I can't spell. Sometimes I have more fun all by myself than with other kids.

I can have as much fun as I want today.
I don't really need someone to help me.

HOW I SEE A SITUATION IS UP TO ME.

Have you ever been sure you saw a grey car that your mom said she thought was green? You wonder if your eyes were playing tricks on you. Eyes don't always see the same things. If my mind was on something really important to me when a car went by, I might not have seen its real color at all.

Sometimes I think someone is making a face at me when she really wasn't. I think sometimes this happens because I was expecting her to act that way. Like one day I was sure that an older kid at my bus stop was making fun of me, but my mother said he was laughing at something down the street behind me. My eyes and mind can play tricks on me.

*Today I'll look at everyone and everything
around me very carefully before making
up my mind about what I am seeing.*

ALL THAT IS NECESSARY TO MAKE THIS WORLD
A BETTER PLACE TO LIVE IS TO LOVE.
–ISADORA DUNCAN

Molly didn't get to come to our school Halloween party because she was sick, so Mrs. Smith sent some pumpkin sugar cookies home with Molly's brother. I wonder if she was too sick to eat them. Mother said that even if she couldn't eat them, they might have made her feel lots better. She said that when somebody does something really nice for us when we are sick, it helps us feel better. Knowing we're really missed and loved helps us heal.

I guess this means I can help someone who's sick by being thoughtful toward them.

Today I'll try to be really kind and considerate.

MAY

BEING LONELY CAN PUSH US TOWARD NEW FRIENDS.

Some days it just seems all my friends are gone. Last week, Suzanne was at her grandmother's house all week long. And Jackie was at the dentist. And Roberta was sick with the flu for three days. I was lonely and bored. Having someone to play with is really important.

I am not the only one who gets lonely. My stepdad says feeling lonely is pretty common. When I was at the park last week, I noticed a girl who was by herself all afternoon. I wonder now if she was lonely. If I see her the next time I go, maybe I'll ask her to play on the slide. That way maybe I'll have another friend to play with when Suzanne and Jackie and Roberta aren't around.

If I dread being alone, I can call up
or reach out to someone new.

NEEDING HELP IS ONE WAY OF
HONORING OTHER PEOPLE'S SKILLS.

Do you enjoy helping out a friend? My best friend Sara may not get promoted into seventh grade if she doesn't get better grades in math and science. I overheard Mr. Justice speak to her about it last week. That would be really sad because next year we go to a new school, and she wouldn't be going with our class. I am sure this would affect our friendship.

I am very good in both science and math. In fact, they are probably my best subjects. Maybe I could offer to help her after school. Mom says trading our skills with others is good practice for adulthood. When she bakes, she always makes an extra batch of cookies for Hildy's mom, and Mrs. Spencer does errands for Mom on Tuesdays. They both get some help this way. Mom says I should try to think of what Sara might be able to help me with. I have noticed that she can braid hair really well. And my hair is long enough now for a braid.

I will offer my help to a friend today and see how it feels.

EVEN THOUGH I CAN'T SOLVE YOUR PROBLEMS,
I WILL BE THERE AS YOUR SOUNDING BOARD
WHENEVER YOU NEED ME.
–SANDRA K. LAMBERSON

When something bothers you, do you ever talk it over? Last week I was really upset because my dad canceled our trip to the amusement park. That's two weeks in a row he changed his mind about taking me someplace. I told Mom, and she said I should tell him how I feel. I'm afraid to do that. I'm afraid he'll do it again this week, especially if he knows I'm mad. Now that he doesn't live with us, maybe he'll just stop coming at all.

Betsy's dad doesn't live at her house either. Her dad only visits once in a while. I asked her if he ever changed his mind about something she counted on doing and she said yes. We talked about it for a long time and then I felt better. It's hard to have my dad living somewhere else . . . but it helps to have Betsy to talk about it with.

I will talk with a friend today if something is upsetting me.

COMPROMISE IS A GROWN UP WAY TO HANDLE DIFFERENCES.

Taking turns is important. I'm glad my grandmother lives with us because she told me how important this was before I started school. I won't mention names, but one of the girls in my class never wants to take turns, and no one wants to play with her. I'm glad nobody feels that way about me.

Of course, I don't always like to take turns either. For instance, when I trip during jump rope, I want another turn right away. The teacher says, "No dice." What a weird saying that is. But rules are rules! I have to go to the end of the line. Taking turns is right for all of us, I guess.

I will have an opportunity to take my turn
in something soon. I won't argue about it.
Even if I don't want to be last, I won't argue!

IT'S A SIMPLE FORMULA:
DO YOUR BEST AND SOMEBODY MIGHT LIKE IT.
–DOROTHY BAKER

Are you as well-behaved as your mother wants you to be? For instance, would you feel okay having your mother watch you during the day? I know that sometimes I do mean things that I wouldn't want my mother to see.

Kyle, one of the boys in my room at school, is pretty mean all the time. I wonder what his mother taught him. I'll bet she doesn't know how he acts. I wonder if he ever feels afraid she'll find out.

Worrying about whether my mom will find out taught me to think twice before doing many of the things that pop into my head. I guess that's good.

I will ask myself, "Would my mother be proud of me today if she could see me?"

HELPING SOMEONE ELSE MAKES THE WORLD A KINDER PLACE.

No matter where I go today, I'll see someone who needs some kind of help. Maybe the neighbor can't bend over very well to reach her newspaper in the bushes. Maybe the little girl next door is learning to ride her bike or trying to catch a beach ball, and I can help by showing her how I do it. Lots of mornings Mom is in a hurry to get my breakfast so she can get to work on time. I can help by putting the milk away, the dishes in the sink, and by wiping off the table.

Helping others doesn't take a lot of time. I can help in lots of ways if I really want to. Maybe I can start by asking Mom what I can do for her right after she has helped me zip up my dress.

If I want to be really helpful today,
I'll make sure to ask how I can help.

To cure jealousy is to see it for
what it is, a dissatisfaction with self.
–Joan Didion

It seems that no matter how good I am at math or how many library books I've read or how quickly I get picked for a side at recess, I always wish I was the very best. Usually, some other boy or girl seems to be better than me at everything! Adults say that's just how it is. They also say I need to learn I'm good enough just as I am.

Wanting to be as good as Abbey in my reading class or as fast as Tom when we're running a race isn't wrong, but maybe I can learn to be glad for them instead of sorry for me. They must have practiced a lot to be so good. Maybe my feelings are telling me what's important to me, and I can set a goal for myself about practicing.

I will remember that if there's something I want to achieve, I can work at it. If I feel better about myself and my goals, maybe I'll be happier about others' success.

SHOWING RESPECT AND LOVE
FOR OTHERS EXERCISES MY HEART.

It is really easy to love an innocent kitten. Kittens are so soft and willing to cuddle! It is pretty easy to love a newborn baby too, because it's innocent and not really able to hurt you. Not all individuals in our lives are easily loved, however. And that's okay. Sometimes we have to steer clear of people who have hurt us. I stay as far away from Bobby, the new kid on our block, as I can. He has a temper!

Mom says learning to show respect and love for people who treat me kindly are good habits to develop. She says the more I practice this, the easier it becomes. Practice makes everything better, she says. She reminds me that my soccer playing got lots better when I practiced. My expressions of love and respect will flow more easily from me with practice too, she says. She calls it *exercising the heart*. I like that idea.

I will look for opportunities to exercise my heart today.

COMPROMISE IS PART OF GETTING ALONG WITH OTHERS.

My dad always says, "It's the human condition to want everything your own way." But getting your own way all the time isn't even a possibility in most families. For instance, do you get mad when your mom says you and your brother have to take turns riding in the backseat of her van? Deciding who gets to go first when the class is playing T-ball can cause an argument too. Taking turns is the only fair way, isn't it? Not always having to be first in line means you're growing up. It means you're learning to compromise. Mom says grownups compromise all the time, especially when they're solving problems at work.

You will have a chance to compromise with a friend today, probably while playing a game. Try it and see how grown up it makes you feel.

I will practice compromising with my sister and a friend.

SOMETIMES THERE IS NO CLEAR ANSWER TO THE QUESTION "WHY?"

I can't understand why bad things happen to people. Why did Rachel's baby brother die? Megan says God punishes people, so maybe the baby did something bad? My grandfather says this isn't true. He says God never punishes us, that no matter what we do, God never stops loving us. But then why do bad things happen? It isn't easy to understand.

Some things just happen, my dad says. It just isn't possible to understand why bad things happen.

*If something bad happens to me or to someone
I love, I won't think of it as punishment.*

HOW WE SEE OURSELVES ISN'T ALWAYS ACCURATE.
−MARGE REED

Do you like how you look when you stand in front of the mirror? Lots of kids−even lots of adults−are very picky about how they look. My brother Jason thinks he's too short. I know this because I heard him complain to Dad. My sister thinks her hair is ugly. It's pretty curly, but I like it. Being too fat or having too many freckles bothers some kids. None of us is perfect, I guess.

My parents say that being short or fat or having lots of pimples doesn't affect what we're like on the inside. And that the inside is what's most important.

How we act and think shows our insides. On the inside, are we kind? patient? generous? Expressing important inside qualities is what counts, not our freckles or fat legs.

I will practice making my insides even better today.
Then I'll express who I really am.

BLAMING OTHERS COMES SO NATURALLY.

I couldn't find my pencil box at school yesterday, and I was really sure that Sophie had taken it. After telling my teacher what I thought Sophie had done, I found my box under the red table. Too often, I blame someone else when I can't find something. Mom gets upset when I do this. My teacher was kind of disappointed too. I wonder why I did that?

I get blamed for things too. When Joey lost his hat, he accused me of putting it somewhere. Then he found it under his bed! Mom even thought I had hidden her purse for a joke, but then she remembered leaving it in the car.

It is not right to blame somebody else for my own mistakes.
If I lose something, I will try to remember what
I did with it instead of blaming someone else.

EVERY PERSON IS YOUR TEACHER.
–FLORENCE SCOVEL SHINN

Does your mother ever have to remind you that everyone in your life is very special? Once in a while, I just don't like my sister. I have even wished she had never been born. And then I felt really scared for wishing it. Has that ever happened to you? It's hard to remember she is special when she breaks my hairbrush just before I need to use it, or when she gets into my favorite markers.

Mom says every single one of us is special to God and that means we are special to each other too. My sister made a beautiful drawing for me, and sometimes on hard days she can make me laugh in a way that no one else can. It's harder to understand what's so special about people I don't like. But Dad says I can learn kindness from the mean-spirited and generosity from those who are selfish.

I will have lots of people around me today.
I can learn something from each one of them.

TALKING ABOUT WHAT
BOTHERS ME USUALLY SHRINKS IT.

Almost every day something happens that bothers me a little. For instance, yesterday my dad seemed mad at me for no reason at all. He didn't smile once while we were eating dinner. He didn't really talk to any of us. After we finished eating, I asked my mother if Dad was mad at me. She said he was just upset about something that happened at work.

It is really important to talk my feelings over with Mom or another grownup or a friend. Just talking to somebody about how I feel helps me feel a little better. I'm glad Dad wasn't mad at me, though. I gave him a big hug right after the talk I had with Mom. He kind of smiled then.

If I am upset about anything, I'll make sure I don't keep it to myself. Talking it over changes how I feel.

TEACHING IS THE ROYAL ROAD TO LEARNING.
–JESSAMYN WEST

Did you know that our teachers aren't just the ones we have at school? Jacob's mom said that everyone who speaks to us every single day is actually one of our teachers. What a funny idea this is. How can my friend Samantha be a teacher? She's younger than me. But Hank's mom says we learn from one another all the time. For instance, we learn what not to do sometimes. I sure don't want to sass the neighbor like Leah did. She got into lots of trouble. That taught me a lesson.

I wonder if this means I'm my sister Julia's teacher. She always wants to do what I'm doing. I better think about what I'm teaching her.

I will be as good a teacher as I can be.

HAPPINESS COMES FROM HAVING A POSITIVE ATTITUDE.

Making the decision to be happy when something crummy happens is pretty hard. I had an opportunity to try this last week, but I didn't do so well. First, my dog Corky disappeared. I was sure he had been stolen because he is so cute. I frantically looked for him all over the neighborhood. My grandmother came for a visit, but I couldn't stop worrying and looking. She left before I had a chance to talk to her. I didn't even thank her for the birthday present she brought because my mind was filled up with pictures of Corky and my fear that he would be forever gone. That night after supper a man came to the door with Corky. So all my worries had been for nothing and I'd ignored my grandmother when she was here specially to visit me.

I have learned, though, that some situations can't keep me from feeling happy. When Mom forgot to buy my favorite dessert, it didn't keep me from laughing over the silly stuff my baby sister did when we were having dinner. Last night, she poured her peas all over her head.

I will attempt to be happy in most situations today.
It may take some effort.

THANKS-GIVING CAN HAPPEN A LITTLE BIT EVERY DAY.

There are hundreds of ways to say thanks. I can simply say *thank you* to everyone who does something kind for me. For instance, when my baby-sitter offers to check my homework, I can say thanks. Maybe she'll help me get an A on the assignment! I can offer to help my little sister braid her hair, just like my stepdad used to help me. There are lots of opportunities. I can even take a little gift to the neighbor who has been kind enough to return all my balls that have fallen into her yard.

One of the ways my mom taught me to say thanks is through prayers. She says thanking God for helping me out every day is a wonderful way to show my thanks. I think I will tell her how thankful I am that she's my mother.

I will be quick about showing my thanks today.

EVERY SKILL TAKES PRACTICE.
–SUSAN ATCHLEY EBAUGH

Every teacher I've ever had said we have to practice skills we want to be good at. That's what my parents say too. Mom is always asking me to practice my spelling words. Sometimes I even ask her to help me practice my subtraction tables. Since I started to take piano lessons, I have to practice piano thirty minutes every night. I don't have very much time to watch TV anymore. That doesn't seem to bother my mom at all.

I really want to read at a higher grade level, so I make sure I read at least a half hour every day. My brother likes hockey–he goes to practice a lot, and I can see what a good skater he's becoming.

❊

I will practice the things that are important to me:
I want to be a good reader and a good piano player!

ILLNESS CAN HAPPEN TO ANYONE, ANYTIME.

Most people feel sick occasionally. My mother stays home from work once in a while when she gets a bad headache. Sometimes she has to miss work because my baby brother is really sick with a temperature. I get a stomachache when I get too hot. Some kids can't drink milk because it upsets their stomachs. Since ice cream is made from milk, I wonder, does that mean they can't ever eat ice cream? What bad luck!

Feeling sick once in a while can happen because we need to rest more. Sometimes I play too hard and then stay up really late at night. Sometimes I catch colds this way. Sickness can be caused by many things, but usually resting and eating healthy foods make me get well.

I will rest well and eat healthy so I can feel good.

GROWING UP GOES HAND IN HAND WITH BECOMING MORE RESPONSIBLE.

As you get older, you are given more responsibility. What does that actually mean? If you ask a teacher, she will probably say it means she can depend on you to erase the boards very carefully if that's your assigned job. Or maybe it means she can trust you to go down to the principal's office to get something without supervision.

Mom says being more responsible means that as I get older, she can count on me watching the baby. She can trust me to make my bed without her having to come in and check my room. Learning to be more responsible is one of the things that's expected of me when I grow up.

*I will try to show Mom and my teacher
that I am very responsible today.*

ARE YOU A GOOD SPORT WHEN SITUATIONS DON'T TURN OUT AS YOU HAD HOPED?

Life seldom happens in exactly the way we envisioned it. In fact, my mom has a great saying. She says, "Life is what happens while you are making other plans." This is certainly what happened to me last week. First of all, I had asked Grace to come for an overnight. At the last minute, she cancelled because her grandmother unexpectedly came for a visit. The next day, I had planned to bicycle to the park for the opening of Monkey Island. It rained. But that's not all. On Sunday, my dad had promised he would come over and take my little brother and me to dinner. He didn't. Mom felt sad for us, so she took us to Burger King, which was fun, but I was disappointed.

Accepting whatever happens as okay takes effort. Mom says she struggles with this too. But she says the better we get at it when we are young, the easier our lives will be when we grow up.

I may as well enjoy whatever happens
today unless it is something I can change.

NOT EVERYTHING THAT GOES ACROSS MY BRAIN NEEDS TO COME OUT OF MY MOUTH.

I get myself into trouble pretty often because I don't stay quiet when I should. My thoughts sometimes tell me to criticize or make fun of someone. Do your thoughts push you to make a mean comment to a friend when she doesn't do something the way you like to do it? What happens next? If your experience is like mine, you end up without your friend to play with because she went home hurt or angry.

Probably your mom and your dad told you to try being quiet rather than doing what your thoughts tell you to do. Everybody says things they wish they hadn't. When my dad yelled about the yard not being raked, he was sorry and apologized. I bet he wished he'd kept his mouth shut then.

Today, I will be really quiet and think
before I say anything I might be sorry for.

I HAVE ACCEPTED FEAR AS A PART OF LIFE.
–ERICA JONG

What are you most afraid of? Have you ever thought about this? Tommy, my baby brother, is afraid of shadows. My dad says he's afraid he will get sick and have to quit working like Grandpa did. My grandmother says she was afraid of people, getting a job, and dating boys when she was younger, but now she lets God have her fears, and they seem to disappear. I'm afraid my mother will start drinking again.

At school last week we talked about fear. I enjoyed the discussion. Mr. Penny said people sometimes get afraid because they forget to tell others what is bothering them. He says if we tell someone what fear is in our minds, it will help it to disintegrate. I've thought about telling God my fears, like Grandma does. I notice when I talk to Mom or Dad about my fears, I feel less afraid.

*I think everybody has fear. If I feel it today,
I will talk it over with an adult or God.*

IF YOU HAVE MADE MISTAKES, EVEN SERIOUS ONES,
THERE IS ALWAYS ANOTHER CHANCE FOR YOU.
–MARY PICKFORD

Making mistakes is part of living, according to my teacher Ms. Banks. She says that no one can expect to be perfect in everything all of the time. Even though she knows all of the words in our books, she even mispronounces one sometimes because she's thinking about something else. Doing our best is what really matters, she says.

I don't always do my best. Sometimes I watch television instead of studying for a test in math. When I miss some problems in class the next day, I know why. This morning I didn't make my bed very well, either. I just threw the covers over my pillow and left all of my stuffed animals on the floor, and I didn't really like coming home later to that mess. I always tell my mother I will try harder from now on.

*Each day I can work on doing my best in something.
Being perfect isn't so important, but trying to be better is.*

RESPECT YOURSELF . . . AND OTHERS.

I hate it when someone calls me a "'fraidy cat." Don't you? Mother says it bothers me because it's embarrassing to be made fun of. She also says that the person who is making fun of me is no doubt scared of many things. They feel better when others are afraid too, she says. Even adults do this, I've noticed.

I never see my parents do this to each other or anyone else, either. So it's possible to be a person who doesn't make fun of others and who is always respectful. That's the kind of person I would rather be. Some things may still make me afraid, but I don't have to make others feel afraid too. Using my mom as a model can help me be more respectful of others.

Today will be my chance to ignore it if someone makes fun of me. I can make sure I don't make fun of someone else too.

I DON'T ALWAYS KNOW WHAT I WANT,
BUT I DO KNOW WHAT I DON'T WANT.
–HELEN NEUJAHR

Do you ever dream about who you may want to be when you grow up? Most kids do. My friend Holly wants to be a doctor like our neighbor Dr. Russell. Her brother says he wants to draw plans for houses and other buildings. That's what his dad does. There are so many people and jobs to choose from! You can work outdoors or indoors. You can have the kind of job where you wear a uniform, like a bus driver or pilot. My cousin Alison is a pilot. She flies planes all over the world. Being a teacher like Melissa's mom looks like fun too. I would really like the summer vacations.

Thinking about what you like to do best will help you know what to do when you grow up. The happiest people are the ones who enjoy what they do.

I can have fun deciding what to do when I grow up.
I will pretend I am already grown up and
see what comes first to my mind.

TO BE COURAGEOUS IS TO BE FILLED
WITH THE STRENGTH OF GODPOWER.
–MARY HELEN SMITH

Courage is a pretty important word. My teacher asked us to draw pictures of courage, and I drew one showing a girl climbing a tree to rescue her cat, who was afraid of the dog chasing it. My friend Joannie drew a picture of a big girl yelling at a group of mean-looking kids who were chasing a little girl.

My Sunday School teacher said courage is when you put your own fear aside for a time. She says it helps to ask God to feel brave in those scary situations. I think everyone is afraid some of the time. My dad says he is even afraid occasionally. He also said that praying helps him.

*If I even feel a little bit afraid, I will ask
God to help me have more courage.*

SOMETIMES I THINK I AM THE
LUCKIEST PERSON IN THE WORLD.
–JANE FONDA

Do you ever wish you were somebody else? Last week I really wanted to be Molly because she got a new bike. This morning I want to be my baby sister because she gets to stay home. I have to go out in the cold, rainy weather to school. Wanting to be someone else instead of being glad I'm me is natural. Not many girls think they are lucky to be who they are.

Have you ever heard your mom say she wishes she were Vanna White because Vanna has really beautiful clothes? That is what Tiffany's mom wishes. It is not wrong, really, to want to be somebody else. But it is really important to realize I'm exactly who I need to be already. God only made one of each of us, so we're all unique and important. My aunt often says, "Turn your eyes toward all that you have, rather than toward what you don't have." When I do this, I can see many ways in which I am lucky.

I will remember that I am who God wants me to be.
Sometimes I just need to remember how lucky I am.

WE ALL HAVE DARK DAYS OF FEAR AND DOUBT.
—JoAnn Reed

My dreams wake me up some nights. They seem so real. Once I dreamed we had moved away to a new house in a new town. I didn't know anybody in my class at school, and whenever I walked into a room, it went dead silent and everybody turned away from me. Was I ever glad when I woke up and went to the bathroom! I could see it was the same old house, which meant my dream was not true and I didn't need to be afraid.

My dreams can help me sometimes, Mother says. They can show me what was on my mind before I went to sleep. Maybe I was feeling afraid about something when I went to bed that night. My dream was about fear, but when I woke up, everything was okay. Knowing that things are okay is a good feeling.

No matter what may happen today, it will be okay, Mother says. She or someone else will help me if I need it.

HELPFULNESS IS A WONDERFUL QUALITY.

There are many, many ways to help other people. Who is one of the most important people to help? Did you think of your mom or dad? You probably did. Sometimes, parents ask for help, but you don't have to wait for them to ask. It's even better if you just offer to help. It makes parents so happy when you offer without being asked. Offering is a very grown-up thing to do.

One of the first things you can do in the mornings is to help make breakfast instead of just waiting for your mom to do it. Even something little like that is a help. Also, you can bring your mom or dad the brush or comb so they can braid your hair before you leave for school.

Even in really little ways, I can help my mom or dad.
That will make them so happy.

TIME WILL BRING THE GOOD TO US
AS WELL AS TAKE AWAY THE BAD.
–AMY E. DEAN

When I'm doing homework or sweeping the kitchen floor or putting the supper dishes in the dishwasher, time seems to drag. All I think about is getting done, and the more I think about that, the longer it seems to take to finish whatever I have to do.

But time goes by quickly when I'm at a movie, at the park, or over at a friend's house playing with her toys. Playing a game on the computer makes time whiz by too. Isn't it weird that time goes by slowly sometimes and quickly at other times?

Mr. Hazzard, my teacher, says that time doesn't change. It's how I think about what I'm doing that changes.

Slow time, speedy time . . . I will try to enjoy it all.

JUNE

LIFE IS ABOUT AVOIDING JEALOUSY, OVERCOMING
IGNORANCE, AND BUILDING CONFIDENCE.
–KATIE LEICHT

I had dinner with my dad last night. He noticed I was
often quick to say I couldn't do something that my
friends were all good at. He asked me how I felt about
my abilities. I told him I was scared a lot of the time
and embarrassed when I couldn't keep up.

I'm not as embarrassed about feeling uncomfortable
now that I know he felt the same way when he was
younger. The first thing we are going to do is work
together on inline skating. He said he puts little messages on his mirror when he is trying to change how
he is feeling about something. He wrote one out for me:

> Dear Kaitlin,
> You are every bit as good as you need to be in
> every activity. Trust me. Believe me.
> > Love,
> > Dad

I believe I can do whatever I need to do today.

SHY FEELINGS ARE COMMON.

Walking onto the school yard where a bunch of kids are already gathered can be hard to do sometimes, especially if there's someone I don't know in the group. I feel a little shy some days. Is there anything wrong with that? I don't like to feel shy, but even moms and dads feel shy sometimes. Just ask them.

What is it that makes me feel shy? Maybe I had a bad dream during the night and it made me a little upset. Or I had a fight with Mom about what I was going to wear to school. Really small things that aren't even important can make me a bit upset, and these can then cause me to feel shy. Feeling shy is very normal. Everybody feels it part of the time, even the most popular girl in the class.

*If I feel shy today, I will remember
that everyone feels shy sometimes.*

MAKING A MISTAKE CAN TEACH ME SOMETHING.

I make many mistakes every day, like everyone else. Some are little ones. Maybe I forgot to brush my teeth before leaving the house, or I put on my old sneakers instead of my new ones when I was getting ready for school because I forgot it was Friday and not Saturday.

Do you ever make mistakes when you're doing addition? That's a bigger mistake, I think. When I know the right answer, it really makes me mad when I miss. I guess I hurry too much sometimes. Lots of mistakes happen when I hurry. Adults even make mistakes when they hurry. Last week my mom went off to work so fast that she forgot her purse. She had to borrow money when she got there for parking.

If I find myself making mistakes,
it may mean that I need to slow down.

BEING THANKFUL IS A GOOD PRACTICE.

Our lives are full of things to be thankful for. We have a school to go to. There's fruit in the refrigerator. Having shoes to wear, especially when it's chilly out, is another thing to be thankful for. Even if I am wearing a skirt that's old, I still have clothes to cover my body. There are children in the world who have to go without shoes and maybe coats too, even when it is cold.

We don't always have all the toys we want. At least that's true for me. I have been wanting a Barbie computer game since my last birthday. And I didn't get my Rollerblades replaced until last week. They were stolen three months ago! But I have balls and crayons and stuffed animals and lots of neighbor kids to play with. Having a bed to safely fall asleep in at night is worth a lot of thanks too. If I look around, outdoors and inside, I can see lots of things to be thankful for.

Making a list of all the things I can be thankful for will be fun. I wonder if I can come up with one hundred things?

WANTING TO BE NOTICED IS OKAY.

When I wear a new dress to school or put on my patent leather shoes to go to the movie with Jennifer and Emily, I hope someone notices and tells me they like what I am wearing. My grandfather says it's normal to want others to notice us. He also says it's normal to not always notice what others are wearing or doing, so I shouldn't expect my friends to always notice me. I'm glad he lives with us because he explains many things to me.

Sometimes I get loud when I want others' attention. Dad pointed out to me that I seem to get bossy and loud when my brother or a friend hasn't asked me to play. When I want others to notice me, for whatever reason, and they are too busy with someone else, I feel left out. I even wonder if they can't see me! Isn't that silly? I am sure I haven't really disappeared.

Mom suggested I try noticing someone else today.
Then I won't feel so bad if no one notices me.

HAPPINESS IS OFTEN CLOSE AT HAND.

What makes you happy? Does having your mother wake you up for school make you happy? Does having your favorite warm cookies waiting for you when you get home from school make you happy? I feel happy when I have done something nice for Grandma and she gives me a big hug. I am really glad she lives with us.

My mother says I have a tendency to notice what I don't have rather than all that I do have. I am working on this, and when I look at my world this way, I do see many reasons to be happy. Last night I drifted off to dreamland listening to Beethoven and curling up with my favorite stuffed animal. Today my mom is picking me up at school. All those things make my heart happy.

*Today I will look for, ask for, go after, and
pay attention to the happy moments in my life.*

WORRYING ISN'T USEFUL.

Moms worry that kids may get hurt on the playground. And sometimes we do. Both dads and moms worry when we're on our bikes after dark. And that can be dangerous, especially if we aren't wearing reflective clothes and don't have lights.

Do you worry much? Sometimes I worry if a certain friend really likes me or if I will remember all the multiplication tables for the big test. Even teachers worry. Ms. Hanson said she worried Monday morning that she would be late for school because her car wouldn't start. She called her brother for help, she said.

Even though most people worry about something, it never helps. In fact, it can make things worse. One time I worried so much about a spelling test that I couldn't remember a bunch of words.

Just because most people worry doesn't mean it's useful.
I will try to spend my energy in better ways.

SLOWING DOWN CAN ACTUALLY SAVE A LOT OF TIME.
–ROBYN HALSEMA

Do you know what it means to be impulsive? That's a pretty big word. You may not hear it very often, but it means doing something too quickly, before thinking it through. I can remember my dad yelling at my brother last week, saying, "Why didn't you think first before slamming the car door?" He was upset because my brother locked his keys in it, and Mom was gone with the spare set.

I showed up at my swim meet last week without my suit because I was in such a hurry to get there. It was a scramble to find a suit in time, and that made me more nervous than usual. Mom says the trick is to slow down. Count to ten or even five before doing things, and your mind will slow down enough to remember what you need to remember. You'll save yourself a lot of trouble.

I will practice slowing down today before I head out the door or before answering any questions.

BEING QUIET CAN HELP US
HEAR IMPORTANT MESSAGES.

Sometimes I get really frustrated because I can't stay in the lines perfectly when I'm coloring a special picture in art class. If I fall off of my bike while Brian is watching, I get upset too. When I am really embarrassed or frustrated, my mind seems like it's going to burst because of all the things I am thinking to myself.

Mom says getting really quiet inside, letting my thoughts just float away, helps. If I get upset with a friend or with Mom because she won't let me go to the park with Amanda, I'll go to my room and get quiet for a while. When I feel calm inside, my peaceful feelings grow stronger than my upset feelings.

Birds get quiet. So do cats and dogs. I will get quiet today when I'm upset and notice how it helps me calm down.

LOVE ONE ANOTHER!

Do you love everyone you know? I don't. Dad says I should try to love everyone. But when Theresa chases me for no reason or when Sandy laughs at me for getting a bad grade in math, I really don't feel like loving them. I don't want to love anybody who isn't really nice to me.

I don't even understand how you can love someone who is mean. Mom says people are only mean when they are afraid. She says mean people even need extra love. That's not easy to do! Mom says if I can't be loving, the next best thing to do is to not hurt them back at least. Maybe I can do that part.

I will not hurt anyone today. Even if somebody is mean to me, I will remember what Mom said about their fear.

THE CHANGE OF ONE SIMPLE BEHAVIOR CAN AFFECT
OTHER BEHAVIORS AND THUS CHANGE MANY THINGS.
–JEAN BAER

Ms. Henry read a story to our class last week. In it, there was a really mean girl named Shelly who chased all the first graders out of the school yard. One of them almost got hit by a car. Shelly got sent home from school. But the next day, she came back and announced over the loudspeaker to the whole school how sorry she was. The principal asked everyone to forgive her.

At first I didn't want them to, but the story showed how she was just very lonely and didn't know how to make friends. After she apologized, one of the other girls in her class asked her to play at recess. The story ended with everyone being happier. The teacher said that was a good lesson for all of us.

*Even if someone is mean to me, I will try to
be kind like the girl was to Shelly in the story.*

DO NOT COMPARE YOURSELF WITH OTHERS. MAKE
YOUR OWN BEAUTIFUL FOOTPRINTS IN THE SNOW.
–BARBARA KIMBALL

Have you ever looked really carefully at yourself in
the mirror? Did you stop to think that there is not another person in the entire world who looks like you
or who has thoughts exactly like you? My grandmother
says that God needed every one of us to be a little bit
different because there were so many jobs to be done
on this earth. I need to remember this, I think, because I often wish I were more like someone else.

Dad says we all make different footprints in the sand
and the snow as a way of emphasizing how important
each of us is. I am not sure I understand what he means,
but he says I will when I grow up. It's one of the truths
that will make sense as I get older. For now, I am trying to be glad I am who I am. One of the things about
me that is different from all of my friends is my ability
to play the piano. I don't even understand this myself.
I can actually play a song after hearing it only a couple
of times. Leah and Holly both wish they could do this.

I will appreciate what I am capable of today.

CAN YOU "ROLL WITH THE PUNCHES?"

Every day something happens that I don't expect. Maybe it rains, and I was going to ride my new bike to school. Or a button comes off a favorite blouse, and I have to wear something else. Maybe I'm really counting on having pancakes for breakfast, but Mom is running late for work and doesn't have time to make them. Things just happen. I can get really upset and pout or even cry, but that won't make the rain stop or put the button back on my blouse.

Being able to accept whatever is happening will probably make me feel better about the rest of the day. Getting no pancakes is not the end of the world! My mom calls it learning to roll with the punches. My aunt, who is a dancer, says it's about meeting life's surprises gracefully. When her ballet teacher changes the beat unexpectedly, it is her job as a dancer to keep up her balance and gracefulness.

Whatever happens today that I don't like isn't such a big deal. Like a dancer, I can stay balanced and graceful despite life's surprises.

TO GET HELP YOU USUALLY MUST ASK FOR IT.

Do you ask for help when you need it, or do you think you should be able to do everything all by yourself? My little sister refuses to let me help her put her shoes on. Dad says that's because of her age.

Some things are really hard for me to do alone, like getting my new jeans buttoned. Putting my bike in the garage when Mom's new car is there can be hard too. She warned me not to scratch it! Even getting all my homework done is hard some days.

It's fine to ask for help. I can ask for help with anything, in fact. If my teacher or my mom thinks I should do it alone, they say so.

There are lots of people around who can help me.
All I have to do is ask!

WE WILL NEVER HEAR ANYONE ELSE'S THOUGHTS IF
WE ARE ONLY LISTENING TO OUR OWN.
—CATHY STONE

What are you thinking about right this very minute? Are you thinking about what you're reading? Are you thinking about school or what your teacher said yesterday about being quiet during class? Maybe you are thinking about your birthday and what you hope grandmother will buy you. Our minds seem to fill up with thoughts, don't they?

There is a time for thinking, and a time for listening. Mom says sometimes we just have to let the thoughts in our mind float away so we can hear what someone is saying. Listening requires being truly interested in what another person thinks and feels. Listening is a very important part of friendship and family life.

I will practice listening today. If I have too many thoughts, I will set them aside so I can hear what a friend is saying.

Nobody can keep you mad but yourself!

Sometimes I get mad at my little brother for messing up my bed right after I have made it. Telling Mom doesn't really help. She thinks I get upset with Sammy too easily. After all, he is only two years old. I have many other reasons for getting mad too. I get mad when my dad forgets to show up for our special night out. That happened twice last month. And I get mad when my friends laugh at me for missing the bus. It happened three times last week.

When I am mad, I can't seem to think of anything else. Being mad just takes over my thoughts. We had a party at school last week, and I was still so mad at my friends that I refused to join in when they were all laughing and popping balloons. When I complained to Mom, she reminded me that nobody can keep me mad. I made that decision all by myself. She said the sooner I learned this piece of wisdom, the better. She is still trying to remember it, she said, and she is thirty-eight years old!

I will remember that if I am mad,
it's my decision, and I can change it.

IT IS WONDERFUL HOW QUICKLY YOU GET USED
TO THINGS, EVEN THE MOST ASTONISHING.
–EDITH NESBITT

Have you recently looked at any pictures of yourself when you were a little girl? It is fun to see how you've changed. When I was a baby, I was totally bald. Now I have lots of hair. It's so long I can wear it in braids, a ponytail, curled, or straight with barrettes. Mom said she thought I would be bald forever because I didn't have any hair by my first birthday!

We change in many ways, not just in how we look. I used to get really scared when Mom turned out my bedroom light. I like the dark now. I can make better pictures in my mind in the dark. My sister used to hate reading because she wasn't very good at it. My aunt took her to a special class where she learned how to sound out words. Now she loves to read. She reads even when it's time to help make our beds.

I will change a lot as I grow up. It is good, occasionally, to notice and celebrate how I've changed and grown.

BEING PART OF A FAMILY IS LIKE PLAYING ON A TEAM.

I get an allowance, but I have to do certain jobs, and I have to do them really well if I want to get paid. Last year, all I had to do was put my toys away before I went to bed. This year, I have to clear the dinner table and sweep the kitchen floor every night. And I have to put my toys away too! Mom says the additional responsibilities are building my character as well as adding to my piggy bank.

My older sister even helps cook. I guess I will, too, when I get older. Mom says everybody has to help out because she doesn't have time to do everything and be a doctor too. She says it's part of being a family, like being on a team together.

I have to do my part around the house.
I'm an important member of the team.

ALL ACTS PERFORMED IN THE WORLD
BEGIN IN THE IMAGINATION.
—BARBARA GRIZZUTI HARRISON

Dreaming isn't just for sleeping. Our imagination, which is where dreams live, can give us the ideas that will point us in certain directions. Samantha's Aunt Karen says we need to have dreams about what we can be when we grow up. She dreamed of being a pilot. And she is! My mom dreamed of being a doctor. She didn't have enough money to go to school that long, so she became a nurse instead and is a good one.

Last week I imagined I was a robot. What a funny day-dream that was! I don't think that's what I will actually be, but maybe I will be a scientist who develops a special kind of robot. Hank, my stepdad, says that dreams indicate where our talents lie. He is exceptionally good at drawing and has been good at that since he was my age. Today he is an architect. I love to draw too. Maybe that job is in my future.

What my mind imagines tells me a lot.
I will notice that today.

CHOOSE TO BE KIND.

Are you always kind to your friends? Probably not. Some days my mother says I act like I woke up on the wrong side of the bed. Those days I'm a grouch toward everyone. Even when my brother or sister or a friend is really nice to me, sometimes I just seem to say mean things or ignore them completely. I don't feel happy when I act this way.

Some of my friends are kind most of the time, especially Shawn. I've never seen her be snotty to anyone. When I'm feeling kind, I don't say mean things to others. Maybe I can pretend to feel kinder, even when I want to be a grouch. When a friend treats me in a kind way, I feel really good. When I decide to treat someone else with kindness, I'll help that person feel good too.

I will spread good feelings by being kind today.

PRAYER IS NOT A SCIENCE.
–MARY McDERMOTT SHIDELER

Praying is something you can do a hundred times a day if you want to. Some people pray as soon as they wake up. Some families pray before they eat every meal. Lots of kids pray before going to sleep. I know a girl who prays before she takes the reading test every Friday. Are there times you would like to pray? You can, you know. Just close your eyes and talk softly to God. No one needs to hear you. You can tell God anything.

Praying makes lots of people feel better. Particularly when you're feeling scared or alone, you'll feel better if you pray. You don't have to tell anyone you are doing it either. You can just quietly, privately, do it.

I will pray today any time I feel like it.
God will always listen.

FRIENDS NOTICE EACH OTHER'S STRENGTHS.

I can do certain things better than Rusty, the girl who lives across the street. I can climb the apple tree much higher than she can. She's a lot better at jumping rope than me, though. I stumble too often. Rusty's mom says each one of us has special abilities, so we can do at least one thing better than anyone else. Reading and playing Scrabble are also things I am really good at.

If my friend Sara needs help in something I'm good at, it's fun for me to help her. Then I can ask her for help with math in return. She nearly always gets a perfect score when we have a math lesson. Helping one another makes all of us a little bit better at everything. That's what friends are for.

I may want some help today with math or riding my new bike. Have I helped a friend lately? If I have, it'll be easier to ask her to help me now.

DO YOU GET THE ATTENTION YOU FEEL YOU DESERVE?

It isn't unusual to want a lot of attention. When I have done my homework for math, then I have reason to raise my hand and I get a lot of attention from Mr. Schmidt. He really appreciates it when we come to class ready to do the work. I get my mom's attention too, when I clean up the family room without being asked. Last week she gave me a special treat, money for another book in the *Goosebumps* series, because I had helped in so many ways without being asked.

I can't say I get all of the attention I want. Some days I want my dad to notice how well-mannered I am at breakfast, but he doesn't. His nose is in the paper.

Ms. Henry, my Brownie leader, says attention is often deserved but not received. She gave each of us the assignment to offer positive attention to a friend during the week so we could report back to the troop on what happened. I loved doing it. I plan to do it a lot.

I will look for reasons to offer positive attention today.
I may get some in return!

FEELING SHY IS COMMON.

Starting at a new school is not the easiest thing to do. I had to do it twice last year! Going by myself to the YWCA for swimming lessons takes courage too. Even going to my cousin's tenth birthday party, where I won't know any of the kids but her, scares me a little. Why do I have all of these feelings?

Dad says it's because I am shy. He says nearly everybody feels shy when they go someplace for the first time. Even he felt shy when he started his new job at the phone company. I'm just like everyone else, I guess. That makes me feel a little bit better.

Today I will remember that I'm no different from all my friends. We are all shy some of the time.

EVEN ON A RAINY DAY, I CAN FEEL THE SUNSHINE.
–JILL CLARK

Attitude is a pretty important word. I can remember hearing my mom say, "Watch your attitude if you want to go to the movie." Maybe we can't always remember what attitude means, but we probably do remember having our mom change her mind about letting us go to the park or over to a best friend's house because she didn't like how we were acting. Attitude, when it isn't good, can cause trouble.

Having a good attitude means we are pleasant toward all the kids in the neighborhood. It means we are respectful of everybody who crosses our path. A good attitude keeps us out of trouble. We can have so much more fun playing with our friends when we have a good attitude.

*Having a good attitude is easy–all I have
to do is to think of myself as sunshine, not rain.*

BEING THE NEW GIRL IN CLASS CAN BE HARD.

It's pretty hard for me to go up to a bunch of kids when I don't know any of them. I'm afraid they won't talk to me or worse, they may chase me away. I can remember when my mother started her new job. She had "butterflies" in her stomach, she said. Having butterflies means you are feeling scared on the inside about doing something new.

It's nice to know that everyone has a hard time being the newest person in a group. Do you know what would be a good thing to do? The next time a new girl shows up in your room, go up to her right away and say "hi." She will feel so much braver then.

*If someone new comes into my life today,
I will make her feel welcome. If I am the new
person, I'll remember it's okay to feel nervous.*

STAYING MAD AT A FRIEND HURTS BOTH OF US.

One time I stayed mad at my friend Torry for two years! She had made fun of me at her birthday party in front of all the kids. She told everybody that Ben was my boyfriend, and he was at the party too. I never spoke to her at school or on the playground, and I didn't even go to her eighth birthday party the next year. She asked me to come too.

Staying mad isn't any fun. Even when it seems like we have a good reason for it, it makes life harder. I never knew what to do when a friend I wanted to play with was playing with Torry. I just had to walk away. I'm glad I finally got over being mad. One day I just stopped feeling mad. I don't even know why. Torry seemed glad too.

Mom says life is too short to stay mad.
She says I should talk about being mad, then let it go.
I'm going to work on the "let it go" part.

I CAN'T GET MY WAY ALL THE TIME.

Mom says I get into too many fights with my sister. Does your mom ever say that to you? I wonder why I fight so much. Mom says it's because I want my way too often. I haven't learned how to take turns. But I don't always get my way at school, and I don't fight there. Maybe because I know my teacher is watching me.

Learning to take turns isn't all that easy. Most people, even moms and dads, want everybody to follow their rules. I don't like it when Jody wants to make all the rules. I guess that's why I can't make them all either. Taking turns isn't a rule just for kids!

I will not push my ideas onto anyone today.

HAVE THE COURAGE TO ACT INSTEAD OF REACT.
–DARLENE LARSON JENKS

When a girlfriend makes fun of you, how do you feel? Do you get mad, or pout, or hit her, or maybe refuse to play with her ever again? It isn't very easy to just walk away, is it? My older sister says that only sissies walk away. But really smart grownups say it's better to walk away from a fight than risk getting hurt or hurting someone else. It isn't easy to walk away, maybe, but I can learn to do it.

Fighting with a girlfriend or a brother or a kid at the park I hardly know always upsets me. It's good to know I don't ever have to fight. It's okay to walk away. In fact, sometimes the best thing to do is to walk away. That way nobody gets hurt.

I will not let anybody trick me into fighting
when what I really need to do is walk away.

IT IS OF IMMENSE IMPORTANCE TO
LEARN TO LAUGH AT OURSELVES.
–KATHERINE MANSFIELD

My mom says there are times when laughing isn't using good sense, like when my friend Timmy made a face at our teacher. Sometimes I laugh before I really think about what I am doing. As long as it's done at the right time, laughing is good for us. My grandmother says laughter is particularly good when we've made silly mistakes. She made one last week that we all laughed at. She tried to throw a cup of water out of her car window. Guess what? The window was closed!

Laughing makes me feel bubbly all over. When I laugh at a funny movie or a joke in a book I'm reading, I feel like being nice to everyone I meet. My mother says laughing can even help us get well when we're sick.

I will laugh at the right times today,
but not when it means making fun of someone.

JULY

CHOICES GIVE US A CHANCE
TO PRACTICE GROWING UP.

When both Heidi and Sandy ask me to come for sleep-overs on Saturday night, it's hard to make the choice between them. Heidi has more computer games than Sandy, which makes her house really fun, but Sandy's mom is so funny, and she always makes fudge or brownies or some other dessert for us, and I love that. I don't want to hurt either girl's feelings. It's probably best to go where I was invited first. That would make it fair for everyone, and I wouldn't have to make any excuses.

Not all choices are so easy. One choice I had to make last year was whether to go to my dad's for Christmas or stay home with my mom. He lives in Florida now, and the weather would have been warm. However, my grandmother was going to be at our house, and she really makes me feel good when she is around. Mom said the decision was up to me. This was a very hard choice. What would you have done?

I may have to make a hard choice today.
I will think it through very carefully.

DEATH IS NATURAL.

It isn't very pleasant to think about dying. My foster mom says that's probably because we don't know how it will feel, and we're afraid. Some of my friends have been to funerals, but not me. Have you been to a funeral? Looking at a dead body would be sort of weird, I think. But when I remember that birds and leaves and flowers die, it's easier to understand why people die too.

Some adults believe a part of us never dies. The body dies, but not the part that talks to God. If that is true, then all the dead people are still alive, in a way. I guess my foster parents and I will stay alive too. I like this idea.

I don't have to worry about dying.
I will just keep talking to God.

WHAT MOST OF US WANT IS TO BE HEARD.
–DORY PREVIN

Does it seem that the teacher doesn't notice you very often? Maybe she's always helping Wendy or Kyle or somebody else when you have your hand up. When you can't get her attention, what do you do? Maybe you feel like crying, or you slam your book closed. It's hard not getting attention when you really need it.

What can you do when you need some attention? In school, maybe you can talk to the teacher during recess and tell her how you feel. Or talk it over with your mom. Maybe she can help you. There's something you can do. Sometimes it just takes some thinking or talking to figure it out.

If I need help today from someone,
I will be patient, but I won't give up.

NOBODY LIKES A GROUCH.

Are you frequently a grouch? How do you know? Maybe someone's called you one. My mom is grouchy once in a while, particularly when nobody comes to the breakfast table on time and she's late for work. When kids at school act up, even the teacher gets pretty grouchy. I think being a teacher must be pretty hard. Kids in my class act up all of the time. My dad is a grouch when I leave my bike out all night!

How does it feel to be grouchy? Some people are grouchy so often that I think they must like the feeling. But I don't like how it feels. I would rather smile and laugh than be grouchy. Sometimes I think of Oscar the Grouch and he helps me laugh at myself. This is a good thing to remember.

✼

If I find myself being a grouch today,
I will find a way to lighten up and laugh or smile a bit.

EVERYTHING HAS ITS WONDERS,
EVEN DARKNESS AND SILENCE.
–HELEN KELLER

Do you ever look up at the Big Dipper at night? Isn't it beautiful? When I was younger, I wondered how all the stars got up there and why they didn't fall down. Now I know they stay in place just like the earth does. One day I watched a mother bird feed worms to her babies in a nest, and I wondered how she knew she was supposed to do that. There are so many things to wonder about.

Cats seem to understand they are supposed to chase mice. Dogs know they are supposed to bark if people come into the yard. Birds chirp loudly when you climb the tree they're in. How does everything know what its job is?

I live in a world full of wonders: today I will notice and appreciate its amazing beauty and order.

I CAN CHANGE ONLY MYSELF,
BUT SOMETIMES THAT IS ENOUGH.
–RUTH HUMLECKER

Don't you wish you could make every one of your friends do exactly what you want them to do? Everybody wishes that, my stepmother says. She wishes we all would come to the dinner table on time, just once! Dad wishes we would get our bikes out of the driveway before he comes home from work. The President of the United States wishes every person who owns a gun would lock it away forever.

Changing someone else is hard work. Actually, it can't be done. Sometimes a friend will do what you want her to do, but that doesn't mean you changed her. All it means is that she changed her mind about what she was going to do. Trying to get someone else to change wastes a lot of time. It's a lot easier just to change yourself.

I will work on changing only me today. If I am unhappy with others, maybe I can just change how I see them.

LOVE YOUR FRIENDS—THEY ARE VERY SPECIAL.

How hard is it to think before doing something? Once in a while, it seems there just isn't time to think first. For instance, when Melissa suggested that we ignore Kira at recess because she hadn't shared her cookies with us, I did it before I even thought about it and then felt sorry later. After all, Kira has always been a special friend, and what I did was not loving at all. My mother explained to me that love is about giving to others first, not just getting something from them, and I forgot this. It's difficult to remember this, but it's not impossible.

Each day it's a good idea to think about a way to express love to a friend. Maybe I can help someone in my reading group who is having trouble with phonics. For sure, I can avoid doing something mean. That's another way of being loving.

I will show my love in many ways today.

ASKING FOR HELP IS NOT ALWAYS EASY.

Sometimes the box of toys is too big to move by myself. Maybe the bed is too wide to reach across to pull
the sheets straight. Maybe I keep forgetting how to
spell certain words for my spelling test. Every single
day, there are things I have to do that are too hard
for me to do alone. I'm lucky that I have friends and
family and teachers who can help.

Asking someone for help is a really good idea for another reason too: everyone likes to feel important.
When I get asked for help, I know I'm needed. And
when someone helps me out, I feel cared for. It's a
great two-way deal.

*Today I'll have a chance to show a friend
or a sister that I need her. That's good.*

OPEN HEARTS CAN GET HURT.

Everybody gets her feelings hurt. I especially get my feelings hurt when I am counting on something that doesn't happen the way I've pictured it. I used to pray that my dad would never drink again, but he did. That really hurt my feelings.

I asked Melissa to come over after school. She didn't promise she would, but she didn't say she wouldn't. When the school bell rang, she ran off with Travis and Troy, the new boys in our class. I felt like crying right then and there. In fact, I did cry after I got home.

Last year, Dad forgot Mom's birthday. She got her feelings hurt too. Dad felt really bad. He probably forgot because he was out of town. I bet he doesn't forget this year. Knowing that having hurt feelings is natural should make it easier for me to get over hurting when it happens. But it doesn't. What does seem to help is having a good cry or talking about my feelings with my mom or best friend.

Since I know how it feels to get my feelings hurt,
I will be careful not to hurt anybody's feelings today.

PARENTS' LOVE FOR THEIR CHILDREN RUNS DEEP.

Do you feel you have to be extra good in every way, or your mother won't love you? Lots of days I feel that way, but my mom says she loves me no matter what. She also says she doesn't always like what I do! It's hard for me to understand how she can love me when I have acted really badly. One day I took some money from her purse without asking. That was wrong, and I was sure she'd quit loving me when she found out. But I was wrong. She was mad, but she never quit loving me.

That doesn't mean making mistakes doesn't matter. I still need to do my best, but I don't always. Some days I am really lazy at school. Yesterday I didn't even do all the problems before turning in my math paper. I got tired and quit. It sure is good that Mom loves me anyway. Today I will do better.

No matter what, I am very loved. I will work really hard anyway. That makes Mom happy, and me too.

"IF ONLYS" ARE LONELY.
–MORGAN JENNINGS

Lots of things happen in a normal day that can upset me. For instance, yesterday I couldn't find my favorite pair of shoes, and it was almost time for the bus. All I could think of was "If only I could find my shoes!" Mom said, "That's life." She meant that we can't always have things the way we want them. Growing up means learning to accept things we can't change.

We get lots of opportunities to accept how things happen every day. I am not so bothered by some things that happen. For instance, last week I had counted on going to a movie with Kimberly, but she changed her mind. I was in the middle of a really good book, so I didn't even care. I don't always act this grown up, though. Sometimes when things turn out differently than I had planned, I have a tantrum! At least that's what Mom calls it.

Today I will work at accepting something I can't change.

PATIENCE IS A VIRTUE.

Tolerance is a new word for me. It means *patiently* accepting situations and people as they are. My mom has asked me to "just be patient!" for a few minutes pretty often. Most people struggle when we don't get what we want right away. Being impatient doesn't make me a bad person, but it can make it hard for others to be around me. When my baby sister is hungry, she cries. Mom says she doesn't know how to tolerate the time it takes to get ready to feed her. Even my dad gets impatient if the newspaper carrier is late getting to our house in the mornings.

Learning to be patient and tolerant is something everybody has to learn. Some of us learn it faster and better than others. Some adults haven't ever learned it. Maybe I can be a good example to one of them.

*I will show at least one person that
I am tolerant and patient today.*

GIVE TO THE WORLD THE BEST YOU HAVE,
AND THE BEST WILL COME BACK TO YOU.
–MADELINE BRIDGE

Do you have a special way to show a friend you love her? Maybe you share your book with her. My brother shows his love by helping me with my reading list every week. I help him by making his bed once in a while. Our parents show us by keeping our clothes clean, making sure there's cereal to eat for breakfast, waking us up in time for school, and holding us when we're afraid.

I don't have to do anything really huge to show my love. I can give Mom a special hug when I come home from school, or compliment my brother on how well he's learning to read or on how good he is at baseball. Expressing my love feels good too.

I will see how many times I can show my love today.

BE ABLE TO APOLOGIZE.

Every single day, I say or do something for which I feel sorry or guilty. Sometimes it's a little thing, like making a face behind someone's back. Or I take something that doesn't belong to me. Maybe I yell at Mom or my best friend for no reason at all, except that I'm in a bad mood. I always know when I need to make an apology; I can feel it inside.

If an apology is necessary today, I won't avoid it. The quicker I take care of it, the better I'll feel. The better all of the other people around me will feel too.

If I've hurt someone I love recently, I'm going to let this special person know I'm sorry.

WE CAN'T TAKE ANY CREDIT FOR OUR TALENTS.
IT'S HOW WE USE THEM THAT COUNTS.
—MADELEINE L'ENGLE

My brother can hit a softball really hard and far. He is probably the best player on our school softball team. My dad plays the harmonica. He isn't as good as he wants to be, but he practices a lot. He plays when he's stuck in traffic. Mom thinks he's getting better, but I'm not so sure. I'm not as good at Spanish as the other kids in my group, but the teacher says I'm getting better. I think doing more homework helps.

We're all good at different things. I am best at drawing pictures. In fact, I think I'm the best painter in my room this year. For the last three weeks, one of my pictures has been up on the main hall bulletin board next to the cafeteria. I feel proud and happy every time I walk by it.

I will work on something I am not so good at today.
I can get better. I'll also appreciate
and notice things I'm already good at.

CONFUSION IS A NATURAL HUMAN FEELING.

I get confused sometimes. Last week in school my teacher asked us to hand in our math assignments. I couldn't find mine, and I knew I had finished it the night before. I looked everywhere. I even looked in my lunch box. I was confused. Later in the morning, we had science. Guess what? In the middle of my science book I found my math assignment. I am still confused about this. I hadn't even taken my science book home. How did it get there?

The best thing about confusion, according to my stepdad, is that it reminds me to pay closer attention to what I'm doing each minute. He thinks most confusion comes from not watching very closely. He suggested that the mysterious reappearance of the math paper was probably due to my sticking it in the science book and then thinking it was my math book when I got to school. He could be right. I was really excited to talk to my friend Hannah when I got to school that day. Maybe I wasn't watching very closely.

I will slow down today. I might be able to eliminate my confusion about what is happening that way.

SOME PEOPLE ARE HARDER TO CARE FOR THAN
OTHERS, BUT EVERYONE NEEDS TO BE CARED ABOUT.

Maybe there's someone in my room at school I don't like very much. Does she act like she knows all the answers? Or maybe it's a boy, and he makes fun of the smaller kids. Sometimes there's a kid who even picks on me, and that's no fun at all! It's hard to remember that God loves every single person no matter what they do. But since that is true, maybe I can figure out how to feel better toward these kids too.

Adults say that someone who beats up on smaller kids is often just afraid himself, so he tries to act real tough. And the girl who always waves her hand to get the teacher's attention just needs to be noticed. Thinking this way helps me feel better about kids I don't like so much. Maybe I can even help them act better by giving them a little extra attention.

The boy or girl I don't like very much is the
person I can help most by being extra nice to.
I can try to love everyone the way God does.

ADMITTING MISTAKES IS A SIGN OF MATURITY.

Mistakes, even big ones like forgetting to ride your bike home from the park, may not be too serious if you admit them before your bike gets stolen. Most mistakes can be corrected if we don't ignore them. What is much worse is to lie about them. I wanted to lie about losing the twenty-dollar bill Mom gave me last week to pay for groceries.

I feel bad when I make a mistake, which is why lying seems like a good solution. I don't want anyone else to know about my mistakes. Sometimes I try so hard to be perfect that I forget nobody is perfect.

Everyone makes mistakes! If I make one today, I will remember that admitting it is the right and grownup thing to do.

BE GENTLE, LIKE A MOTHER CAT WITH HER KITTENS.

It's easy to be gentle when I touch a baby kitten or the little yellow chick I got at Easter time one year. When I get to hold a newborn baby, it's easy to be gentle too. Mom says I can learn to be gentle in other ways as well. I can answer people's questions with a gentle voice. I can speak to my friends and family in a gentle way. I can help set the table for dinner gently too.

Being gentle is more than just a way of touching something. It's a way of thinking and speaking and even listening. It means I'm trying to be soft and full of love. When my mom is soft and loving toward me, I feel special. I can show that kind of softness to others too.

❀

I will be as gentle to those I am
with today as I would be to a baby.

CREATIVITY IS PART OF BEING ALIVE.

There are lots of ways to be creative: drawing a picture of an elephant and picking up pretty leaves on the way home so that I can make a design on paper. My teacher says it's good to be creative. She says everybody is creative in some way. She can play the piano. My brother is learning to tap dance. My mother writes poetry, and my dad tries to put music to her poems with his guitar. He hits a lot of sour notes, though, and that makes us laugh. Mom says creativity is what makes us most alive. And it's fun!

I'll watch how other people are being creative today. Maybe I can even try some new ways to be creative myself.

Today I'll enjoy the world around me. I'll be creative!

EACH DAY PROVIDES ITS OWN GIFTS.
–RUTH P. FREEDMAN

Some days I seem to wake up feeling a little bit troubled. I wonder if my unhappiness is because I had a bad dream I can't remember. Or maybe I know my dad will be upset because I don't want to go to his house this weekend. The more I think about my feelings, the deeper my unhappiness goes. I learned a trick from Grandma, though, that I can always use when I feel unhappy.

First, I get a pencil. Next, I make a list of all the good things that happened yesterday. I could put down the 'A' I got in spelling on my list. I could also mention the good cookies Mom made for dessert. Grandma says when I begin to count up all of the good things that happen, the few things that made me unhappy won't seem so big.

*I will probably be surprised at all the
good things in my life if I write them all down.*

BEING ANGRY WITH FRIENDS IS NOT EASY.

When I have a fight at school or with one of my friends who lives close by, it makes it hard to even see them. That's how I felt after Molly and I fought over who had the most jewelry. It's okay to feel like this for a while. Even adults sometimes feel this way. But I can't stay mad forever. What's the solution?

Deciding to say I'm sorry is not easy, but it's one solution. Asking Mom or Dad for help with working out a solution is another good idea. After talking it over with my dad, I realized I was angry at Molly because she had become so mean in the argument we had. And I realized I had been mean also. My dad promised that if I apologized for my mean words, I would feel better. I practiced saying I'm sorry to one of my stuffed animals. Then, when I saw Molly, I pretended I was still saying it to the stuffed animal, and I got the words out just fine. In no time at all, we were playing again and laughing. The jewelry argument was forgotten.

Being angry happens to everybody.
It's important to find healthy, respectful
ways to talk about anger and then to move on.

SICKNESS HAPPENS TO EVERYONE.

Is someone you know sick? Maybe it is just a case of the flu or a bad cold, and we all know that flu and colds go away in time. Emma's mother has something more serious, though. She was in the hospital for many weeks and is in a nursing home now. Emma says she may not be able to come home for a few months.

It's rather scary when someone I know is sick. Often there isn't very much I can do. My grandmother believes prayer is important. My dad says spending some extra time with Emma right now would be helpful too. Making a special get-well card for Emma's mother, maybe baking some cookies for Emma's family are a couple of things that would help too. According to my mother, the important thing is to extend myself in some way. I should think of something that would make me feel better in this situation, and then do it for my friend.

Being thoughtful when a loved one
is sick is something I can do today.

ATTITUDE AND PERSPECTIVE ARE EVERYTHING.
–KATHY KENDALL

Some people whine and complain all the time. You probably know somebody who does that. My friend Jasmine complains a lot. I don't really like to spend much time with her or with other people who always complain. Their poor attitude ruins my fun. Kids who laugh a lot or maybe play a lot of jokes on others are much more fun to be with. My older sister says kids like that have a better *perspective* on life. That's a big idea, but it means they see life more positively.

I wonder why some people complain so much. My sister Rebecca says that complainers are just afraid. Maybe they're afraid other kids don't like them, or maybe they're afraid they can't learn what everyone else already knows. I know that when I'm afraid or tired, I whine a little bit too.

If someone starts complaining, I will
see what I can do to help her feel better.
Instead of a whiner, I'd rather be a fun kind of girl.

YOUR MIND CAN HELP YOUR BODY
DO LOTS OF THINGS: THINK POSITIVE!

Did you know that you can do almost anything you think you can do? It works like this. Let's say you really want to be able to ride a two-wheel bike. First, imagine yourself riding by imagining just how you get on it. Now imagine yourself pedaling slowly, moving down the street. Don't go too fast. Now put the brakes on and put one foot down on the ground. See, you can do it in your mind. Now it's time to try the real thing!

This is how you can learn to do anything new. Imagine how it will go first. What a neat trick! Look at all the new things you can learn this way.

I will practice in my mind something
I have never done before, and then I'll
try it for real. Today will be pretty exciting.

FEAR AFFECTS EVERY PERSON IN SOME WAY.

Everybody is afraid some of the time. When Mom had to give a speech in front of her club, didn't she say she was scared? And when Jason's dad got arrested for speeding, I bet Jason was afraid his dad might go to jail. Being afraid right before a math test or when the principal comes into the room just as the teacher calls on you to read happens to all of us.

What does being afraid feel like? I get the feeling of butterflies in my stomach. I feel all jumpy inside. Usually I can't eat when I am afraid, either. Stacy says she gets a headache when she's scared. My mom says her hands shake. It seems like something happens to everyone who is scared.

I will not be surprised if something makes me a little bit afraid today. Being scared once in a while is normal.

PRAYING CAN HELP US WHEN
WE ARE SCARED OR CONFUSED.

We don't have to know a certain prayer by heart. We can say something really simple like, "Dear God, please help me not be so afraid right now." And everybody says a prayer sometimes. Praying before eating a meal is called "Saying Grace." Some families always say grace. Saying a prayer like, "Now I lay me down to sleep," when we go to bed at night makes us just like millions of other kids. That's a simple prayer I learned in Sunday School when I was really small.

There is no law that says we have to pray. It's nice that we don't have to do it. It's better if we pray because we want to. Praying is something my father does every morning.

I don't have to wait to pray just when I go to bed.
I can ask God to help me anytime I want to.

GENEROSITY IS A VERY GOOD HABIT TO DEVELOP.

Sharing my toys with my little sister or brother is a nice thing to do. I may not want to share them because I may be afraid a special toy will get broken. But when I remember how good it feels when a friend lets me ride her bike or read her favorite book, I know why it's good for me to share too.

Sharing gets easier the more I do it. I begin to enjoy making other people happy. It begins to make me really happy too. After all, it's more fun to have friends than untouched belongings.

*Today I will let a friend play with one
of my favorite things. Sharing will feel good.*

FIGHTING WITH A FRIEND ALWAYS MAKES ME SAD.

When you can't get your best friend to play the board game you have been asking her to play every day for a week, do you get mad? Maybe she has a good reason for wanting to play something else. Maybe she doesn't know how to play the game you prefer, or has forgotten how to play it. Did you ask her? If you want to spend time with her, why not go ahead and play what she wants instead of fighting over it, or make a deal to take turns getting your way? Fighting is never any fun. At least I don't think so. In fact, fighting makes my stomach upset.

When I'm about to fight over a difference of opinion, sometimes I decide instead to let the other person have her way. It really isn't so bad to give in once in a while. It's better than having an upset stomach!

I don't have to get my way today. It's no big deal.
I'll be as happy or happier if I don't.

PRAISING OTHERS CAN BRING PRAISE BACK TO US.

Having the teacher notice how carefully I wrote my spelling lesson made me feel really good. Doing a really careful job of making my bed, pulling the sheets extra tight, will get noticed by Mom, I hope. Whenever I do a job around the house really well, she usually tells me how glad she is. I love having people notice my good work. Am I different from my friends? Mom says not. She says everyone likes to be praised.

I am sure I'll see a friend do something today that I can praise her for. Sherry is usually the neatest printer in the whole room. Maggie makes us all laugh. Sue can talk to everyone in our class, even the shy and quiet ones.

I'm going to be on the lookout today for reasons to praise others. Maybe someone will praise me too.

WHEN YOU NOTICE WHAT YOU DON'T HAVE,
PAY ATTENTION TO ALL THAT YOU DO.

Do you know what it means to compare yourself to others? It means matching what you have with what they have and deciding who has more. For instance, Judy got a new bike for her birthday. Brad got one for being such a big help while his mom was in the hospital having his baby sister. And I've never had a brand new bike. I got caught up in the unfairness of it without stopping to think that I have a dog and a cat and my friends have neither.

Not everyone has the same number or kinds of things. I guess as long as I have certain things, like a bed to sleep in and plates to put food on and shoes to wear when I go out to play, I'm pretty lucky. You know, some kids don't have nearly as much as I have. Just look around and see what all is in your house and in your bedroom. Lots of stuff. You actually have enough, don't you?

*If I am wishing I had something new today,
maybe I should just count all the clothes, music,
and books I can see in the corner of my closet.*

AUGUST

REACTING WITHOUT THINKING FIRST CAN GET ME INTO TROUBLE.

It isn't always easy to slow down enough to think, particularly when my grouchy brother starts chasing me. Picking up a rock to throw at him seems like the natural thing to do. But what if I hit him, cut him, send him off to the emergency room? Then I will wish I had stopped to think before acting.

Most things that are happening around me don't require my response. Even if someone is being nasty, I don't have to do or say anything back. Can you stop yourself before reacting in a way you'll regret later on?

I will do nothing until I think it over in my mind first.
That will make today an experiment, just like science class.

EVERYONE IS BASHFUL SOMETIMES.

If you've never played with a certain girl before, are you bashful about asking her to jump rope with you? Maybe that hasn't happened to you, but maybe you've tried to find a place to sit in the lunchroom when your friends have filled up their table already. Are you bashful about sitting with a group of kids you don't know very well?

Feeling a little bit scared is what bashfulness is. But there really isn't anything to be scared of. I've been told that we always have a guardian angel who will never leave our side. So even when I end up having to sit by a stranger at lunch or on the bus, I'm not sitting there alone. My "best friend" is right next to me. That's really nice to know.

I will remember that I am not alone even when I am surrounded by kids I don't know. I love knowing my guardian angel is always ready to help me.

CHANGING MY MIND CAN HURT
SOMEONE ELSE'S FEELINGS.

Robyn said she was coming to my house after school, but she hurried off with Rachael as soon as the bell rang. I wonder if she is mad at me? Does this ever happen to you? Making plans with friends can be frustrating. People don't always do what they said they will do.

Mom says this happens sometimes. People just change their minds, but it hurts my feelings when I am not told ahead of time. Now that I know how it makes me feel, I will try hard not to do this to someone else.

Changing my mind at the last minute isn't fair to my friends. I'll try to do all the things I said I would today.

I TRULY WANT TO BE PART OF THE SOLUTION,
NOT PART OF THE PROBLEM.
–KATHY KENDALL

Have you ever heard an adult describe a friend as always seeing the glass as half empty? That sounds weird, but its meaning is simple. It means the friend always sees the negative side of a situation, not the positive side. That person sees only problems, not solutions.

I have three best friends. My problem is that two of my friends don't like each other very much. When I want to have a sleep-over, I have to choose Susan or Kelley but never both. I talked this problem over with Dad, and he suggested that I talk to each girl privately about my feelings and ask them for a solution. I was nervous about doing this at first, but I did it. Guess what? They agreed to try to be better friends to each other. Last week was the first sleep-over with all of us, and we had fun! I can hardly believe it. My dad is pretty smart.

I will try to look for a solution
whenever a problem comes up.

A MIRACLE CAN BE ALMOST ANYTHING.

When we have planned a picnic and it doesn't rain, my grandmother Rinny says, "This is a miracle!" Last week, when I got an A in math even though I'm not very good at multiplying big numbers, I thought, "Wow, a miracle!" Mom says it was a miracle she remembered everything she went to the store to buy because she forgot her list.

I wonder if all these things are really miracles. Does a miracle have to be some big deal? When I fell down the stairs at school and didn't even tear my skirt, I called it a miracle. Mr. Temple, my old art teacher at Sunnyside, said miracles live in our minds. How we see an experience is the miracle, he says.

If everything works out well today, I may think it's a miracle.

BEING NEW TO A CLASSROOM CAN BE INTIMIDATING.

Have you ever been the new girl at school? Maybe you're lucky and have lived in the same house and gone to the same school ever since kindergarten, but poor Janice has been in three schools already. It must be hard to make new friends over and over. But my teacher says we can each help the new person by offering to be her friend right away.

I noticed that Stephanie talked to Janice right away. I bet that made her feel welcome. I wish I had gone up to her right away. Maybe I can invite her over to my house this weekend. Being the new girl can make you feel popular, but it can also be lonely if no one asks you to play.

I will be extra nice to every new girl in my class.
I may have to move someday too.

Where is God?

Some people say that God is everywhere. I wonder if that means God is in the pretty leaf I picked up on the way home from school. Is God also in my angel fish? If God is in everything, why is Shawn so mean? Wouldn't God keep Shawn from chasing the little kids?

Sometimes it is hard to understand how all this works, but some grownups say that God can always help you do the right thing if you ask for help and you really want the help. It seems like a good idea to ask for help. I wonder if all the fish and rabbits and trees ask for help.

Even if I don't understand just how God actually helps us, I can ask God to make my day a happier one.

NEVER LOSE HOPE.

Never lose hope. That's written in big letters on our refrigerator. I'm not sure I understand what it means. I do hope for a lot of things. Like I hope I pass to the next grade in June. I hope I get all A's on my report card. I hope my baby sister learns to leave my dolls alone. I hope my older sister comes back home. She ran away last year to my aunt's house. Mom says that is one hope that might not get answered until my sister gets out of high school.

Having hope means you don't give up. But lots of things I hope for are going to take effort, or they won't really happen. I can't just hope to pass my spelling test. I have to study. I can't even just hope that Stacy will leave my dolls alone. I have to tell her what I expect her to do. Hope doesn't take care of everything without some work from me. But hope makes me feel like all good things are possible.

*I can be hopeful about a lot of things today
but I have to make sure I am doing my work too.*

LAUGHTER CHANGES OUR WHOLE PERSPECTIVE.
–JAN PISHOK

Laughing over a good joke makes my body feel good all over. Does it have that effect on you? Occasionally, I wake up a little sad, or like one day last week, a little scared because I had not finished my science project for school and it was due that day. When I went into the kitchen for breakfast, the first thing I noticed was my cat all tangled up in some yarn. She looked so cute and befuddled that I laughed really hard. Instantly, my fear left me and I felt really good about everything. My project was still unfinished, but I felt calmer about being able to explain that to Mr. Jerome, my teacher.

My grandmother has always said that more laughter could change the direction of the world. I never really understood what she meant. I think I have a better sense of her meaning now.

*I will try to notice how laughing changes
how I see what is happening around me today.*

IT'S GOOD TO TALK ABOUT SAD AND MAD FEELINGS.

Do you ever wish you had kept quiet instead of yelling at your friend? Like when Molly chose someone else to sleep over, did it help me to yell at her? I usually yell or get mad when I am feeling hurt about something. The problem is that my reaction doesn't make me feel any better. Often I feel even worse.

Actually, I can always go to my mom or some other grownup and tell them how I feel. That way I won't need to yell at someone else. It helps to share with someone I can trust when my feelings are hurt. It's a safe way to get rid of them so I can feel happy again.

If I feel angry or hurt, I will talk about it with my mom or aunt first, before I say or do something I may regret later.

THE MORE I FORCE THINGS, THE TOUGHER MY LIFE.
–HELEN NEUJAHR

What makes you mad? Think about this for a minute. Do you get mad when you can't force a friend to play your way? Or when your mom says no to something you want to do? I recently got mad when Tricia didn't ask me to come over after school, especially after I found out she had asked Blythe, the new girl in our class.

Getting mad at others is something everybody does, adults too. I get maddest when others don't do what I want them to. It's like I want to force everybody to let me be their boss. My aunt has a favorite prayer that begins with "God grant me the serenity to accept the things I cannot change." When I bump into something I don't like and can't change, thinking about my aunt's prayer helps me.

I will work on accepting the things I cannot change.

FEARS CHANGE AS WE GROW.

Is there something in particular that you are afraid of? My aunt is afraid of big dogs. When she was a young girl, a German shepherd chased and bit her. He drew blood. Big dogs have been a problem for her ever since. Little kids are sometimes afraid of big kids. Most of the time they don't need to be, but I remember when I was little and a big kid named John beat me up for no reason. I was afraid of big kids for the rest of that year.

Sometimes I'm afraid of the dark, but not every night. Were you afraid the first time you went to the dentist? I was. I was afraid the first day of school too. I cried for about a week before the first day. It seems silly now to think of all the times I used to be afraid. It's nice to grow out of some fears.

I will probably be afraid of something today. I'll try to remember that I won't always fear it.

TO BE TRUSTED BY THOSE WHO LOVE US,
WE NEED TO TELL THE TRUTH.

Sometimes, almost before I realize it, I find I haven't told my mother the truth about why I'm late coming home from school. Once I remember saying that Melinda lost her sweater and I had stayed to help her find it. Was I ever scared when we ran into Melinda's mother at the store and my mother mentioned the lost sweater!

The reason people lie is because they're afraid that telling the truth will get them into trouble. My dad says it works just the opposite of that. If I tell him a lie and he catches me at it, then I'm in trouble for sure. But he promised not to get mad if I always tell the truth, even if what I did was not so good.

*I will tell the truth. Lying makes
my life too complicated, anyway.*

I LIKE TO FEEL GOOD ABOUT MY OWN BEHAVIOR.

I'm not always proud of how I act. When I threw my
tennis ball really hard at the bedroom wall because
my dad said I couldn't go over to Lauren's house, I
knew my behavior was crummy. I'm certain my dad
heard the thud. He didn't say a thing, but he didn't
need to. I felt bad about it anyway.

I don't like feeling bad about my behavior. It affects
everything else I try to do the rest of the day. But
with the help of my grandmother, I have learned that
when I apologize for bad behavior, I feel much better
almost right away! She says there is always a resolu-
tion to the bad feelings we get from our behavior.
Owning them and then making amends for them
changes the rest of the day. I am so glad she taught
me this.

I want to feel good about myself,
so I will take charge of how I behave today.

EACH OF MY DAYS ARE MIRACLES.
–KELLEY VICKSTROM

When I got an A on the spelling test, I called it a miracle. I hadn't even studied. When Mother just barely missed hitting the tiny kitten that ran in front of our car on our way to Stacy's house, she exclaimed, "What a miracle!" One time it quit raining just as we were leaving for church and I was wearing my brand-new sneakers. Richard, my mom's boyfriend, laughed and called that a miracle too.

It sure seems like there are a lot of miracles! My grandfather says miracles happen when we decide to notice the good experiences in our lives. When we do this, it seems like miracles keep happening.

Being happy about what happens today
means I can hope to experience a miracle.

How do you get and give attention?

Wanting my parents to notice my room after I clean it or wishing I would be the first person chosen for a softball team is normal, my teacher says. We all want to be special, and getting attention makes us feel special. But we can't get all the attention we want all of the time. Attention has to be shared, just like so many other things.

Even adults want lots of attention. We're no different from them. So I guess we all need to feel special. Maybe if I make someone else feel special, she will take a turn at making me feel special too. What can I do? Maybe just listen closely or compliment Mary Beth, that will show her I think she's special.

*I will show someone how much I like
her today by paying attention to her.
This would be a very good thing for every person to do.*

JEALOUSY IS A VERY UNCOMFORTABLE FEELING.

What if your best friend gets a beautiful new bike, and it isn't even her birthday? How does her good fortune make you feel? Are you happy for her or are you jealous because your old, beat-up bike is the one your brother used to ride? It's pretty normal to be jealous, to envy what other kids have. My older sister is jealous because her best friend has a really cute boyfriend, and she doesn't have a boyfriend. You may even have heard your mom or dad say they were jealous because the neighbors got a new car. I guess jealousy is everywhere.

If we are jealous, it doesn't mean we are bad, according to my dad, but it's so much better if we can learn to be glad for other people. To do that, it helps to notice what we ourselves have. For instance, I may ride a beater bike, but my Rollerblades are the best on the block. My sister made the cheerleading team, and her best friend didn't. When we appreciate what we do have, it's easier to be happy for what others have or get.

I will try to be glad for all my friends today.

I FEEL WE HAVE PICKED EACH OTHER FROM THE
CROWD AS FELLOW-TRAVELERS.
–JOANNA FIELD

Mother says every friend I have is very important. She
even says the reason for my many different friends is
because of all the things I need to learn. For instance,
Hannah is very pushy and always wants me to do things
her way. She gets me to do things I might not do on
my own, like the day we rollerbladed to the store.
We laughed so much! I'm also learning how to say no
to Hannah when it's something I really don't want to do.

From Joyce I am learning that it's better to share than
to be stingy. She never wants to share anything with
the rest of us. My big sister teaches me many things
too. The first one that comes to mind is how important practice is for learning things. She practices her
piano every day, and she is getting so good!

*Someone will probably learn something
from me today. I wonder what it will be?*

MAKING MISTAKES IS COMMON.

It's a good thing that making mistakes is something everybody does. Otherwise, whenever I made one I would be really embarrassed. Yesterday even my teacher made a mistake: she added up a list of numbers and got the wrong answer. We all had a good laugh over that. Brad told her she better take some homework home. That made her laugh really hard.

Usually I make mistakes when I am doing one thing but thinking about something else. Ms. Carl was probably thinking about going to lunch because the bell had just rung for us to go to the cafeteria. We loved her mistake because it reminded us that nobody is perfect.

I will do my best today in school and at home, but if I make a mistake, I'll know it's okay. I don't have to be perfect.

HARMONY EXISTS IN DIFFERENCE
NO LESS THAN IN LIKENESS.
–MARGARET FULLER

Sometimes Hayley makes me so mad! She always has
to play at her house. She never wants to come to my
house. She says she has more computer games than I
have. I think she does, but it still isn't fair. Maybe I just
have to make another best friend. When I asked Mom
about this, she said I could decide it's okay to play at
Hayley's house all the time.

Disagreements aren't any fun, but sometimes it seems
like we can't avoid them. Maybe I can learn that disagreements aren't so important and that they are a
part of friendships. My mom and dad have disagreements, but they're still married and laugh a lot. I'm
not sure I understand how this works. But it helps me
to think of my disagreements as a small part of a big
picture. The bigger picture includes laughter, fun,
good talks, and great company.

*If I argue with a friend today, I will also
remember how much I care about her.*

FEELING SICK CAN RUIN WHAT YOU HAVE PLANNED.

It's not unusual to have an occasional day when you don't feel so good. Maybe you wake up with a headache or a toothache. Or worse, maybe you have the flu and feel like throwing up. That happened to me last week. Yuck!

If you have planned a special activity, it's really a bummer to be sick. The school picnic is something I hate to miss, and so is a field trip. Being sick may mean I need to get more rest. While I'm in the middle of it, the sick feeling seems like it will last forever, but it never does.

Taking time out for my body to get well is good for everyone. I don't want to spread my germs to others. And I need to remember that the more rest I get, the quicker I'll get well.

If I am not feeling well today, I will stay quiet.
Being sick is not so awful. I can daydream or read a book.

I AM IN GOD'S CARE AND IF I TRUST,
ALL OF MY FEARS WILL SUBSIDE.
—MICHELE FEDDERLY

Everybody feels a little afraid part of the time. A bad storm may make even your older sister a little bit afraid, especially if all the lights go out. Even my dad doesn't like storms. And he says I don't have to be ashamed of being afraid. It will make me feel better if I tell someone how I am feeling. Maybe that person will admit to being afraid, too, and then we'll both feel better.

Being afraid of some things is good. For instance, running across very busy streets should feel scary and make you extremely cautious. If you weren't a little bit afraid, you might run right out in front of a car. That's what my dog did. Being afraid to pet a dog that growls every time you walk by its house is good too. He could bite you. But there is no need to be afraid of everything. Most things really won't hurt us.

Being afraid is okay, but it can become a habit.
I will talk over a fear I have today with an adult.

PEOPLE SEE THINGS VERY INDIVIDUALLY.

If you've ever watched a car accident or a friend falling off a bike, you probably thought you saw exactly what happened. But if someone standing right next to you was watching the same thing, you may have argued over what really happened. That is because we all see things differently.

Each of us see through our own eyes. Miranda and I are always together, so we see the same things all of the time. And we often see things just a little bit differently. Sometimes this drives me crazy, but mostly, I feel like we learn a lot from each other. She always surprises me!

I will let my friend have her own opinion about everything today. I can keep my own opinion too.

WORRYING SOLVES NOTHING.

I am really a worry wart sometimes. A worry wart is someone who worries all the time over really silly things. They worry about the dog getting loose even though they know he is safe in the yard. Or they worry about whether it will rain two weeks from now, when the school picnic is planned.

Do you ever worry about whether a particular friend will stay your best friend forever? Some kids worry that their clothes are not as nice as everyone else's. There are so many things to worry about. But worrying never helps, according to my stepmother Laura. She says it drains our energy!

If I start to worry today, I will just stop.
Worrying won't help you or me. There are a
lot more interesting and better ways to use my energy.

THE FUTURE IS MADE OF THE
SAME STUFF AS THE PRESENT.
–SIMONE WEIL

Do you spend a lot of time thinking about tomorrow or maybe next week? Sometimes I even think about when I'm going to be old enough to get married. My mother says I am missing out on today because I spend so much time thinking about the future. But when my birthday is coming up or maybe Christmas, it's hard not to dream about it. For me, at least.

I guess she is right, though. When my mind is on the future, I am not able to really think about what is happening around me. Just yesterday, I was thinking about planning a sleep-over with Anna while Erin was playing here. It took me a while to realize I was wasting my playtime with Erin by thinking too far ahead.

*It may be hard, but I will just pay attention
to whatever is happening right now.*

THERE WERE DEEP SECRETS HIDDEN
IN MY HEART, NEVER SAID FOR FEAR
OTHERS WOULD SCOFF OR SNEER.
–DEIDRA SARAULT

Do you ever keep secrets from one of your parents? Maybe you got into trouble at your brownie meeting once and you hoped they wouldn't find out. The worst part about keeping that kind of secret is that we worry someone will find out. Every now and then a friend keeps a secret from you. How does that make you feel? Secrets can cause unnecessary trouble, can't they?

But not all secrets are bad. For instance, if your mother tells you what she bought your brother for his birthday and she tells you not to tell, that's a good secret to keep. It isn't always easy to tell the good ones from the bad ones, though. So be careful. If the secret you are keeping makes you feel upset inside, it is probably one you should talk over with a grownup.

My insides will tell me if I am keeping a bad secret today. Mom is someone I can tell. I can tell my teacher too.

HOPE HELPS ME KEEP GOING.

Do you know what it means to have hope? Last year my teacher said we should never give up hope. She said if we had hope, it helped every part of our lives. She told us to sit quietly and make pictures in our minds of what we hoped for. Every day I hope I don't miss any words when my teacher calls on me to read. My mother hopes she gets a new job soon. She isn't very happy at her office. My big sister hopes her boy-friend takes her to the movies.

I wonder what hope does? It seems like it mainly gives me something to put in my mind in place of fear. Hope makes everything seem a little easier. Being quiet and letting my mind and heart fill up with hope makes my world brighter.

I will fill my mind with hope,
especially when I begin to be afraid.

EVERYONE EXPERIENCES SADNESS.

Last week, I was really sad because I lost my favorite pencil coming home from school. It had a Snoopy on top, where the eraser usually is, and my favorite grandmother gave it to me. Probably somebody picked it up and is now using it at home.

I was even sadder when my hamster died. Her name was Hilda. We called her Henry at first, until she had babies! What a joke on us. At least we still have two of her babies. Feeling sad makes me want to just sit by myself in my room or crawl into my mother's lap.

It's okay to be sad. Everyone is sad some of the time.

LOVE IS ALL AROUND US.
–MARIANNE WILLIAMSON

Do you know what it means to love somebody? *Love* is a pretty hard word to explain, isn't it? Even moms and dads and other adults can't always explain it. But most of us know love when we feel it. When your dad surprises the family with a pie from the bakery, isn't that showing love? Another time we can feel love is when a parent or maybe a grandparent tucks us into bed at night, especially if they sit there a while and chat with us.

Love makes me feel cozy and safe inside. Love helps me know that other people want to be close to me. Love is being treated in kind ways. Sometimes love is being held close when I'm scared.

Do you show others that you love them? Do you notice the love coming to you?

I will give love to the important people
in my life today. I will start with my mom.

I DO NOT HAVE TO ALWAYS BE RIGHT!
–MARY ZINK

Why do some people think they have to be right all of the time? I hate hearing my parents argue. They do it a lot too. I don't like to hear Joanie and Rachel argue, either. They are both my best friends, but they don't seem to like each other very much. Arguing makes me a little nervous. Sometimes I want to tell my dad to be quiet, and once I took Joanie's side because Rachel can be really bossy. That didn't make me feel any better, though. Actually, they got mad at me when I took sides. Boy, was I surprised! I wasn't even in the argument.

This is what I notice when I watch an argument: nobody is listening! If each side really listened to the other side, that would help a lot. Sometimes, both sides are a little bit right.

If I disagree with someone today, I will work on listening instead of fighting to be right.

SEPTEMBER

BRAVERY CAN BE A DECISION.

What does it mean to be brave? It might mean we aren't afraid to sleep in the dark. Or it could mean we have studied all the spelling words and are ready for the test on Friday. Being brave can mean we are ready to admit a mistake we made to whoever is around. Being brave means we can face whatever is about to happen. We know we will be okay and that being a little scared is no big deal.

How do you get braver? That's the big question. My stepdad says bravery happens more or less by itself as we get older. Mr. Simpson says praying helps him feel braver. My grandmother says the more we practice being brave, the braver we become. My older sister, Hannah, says she decided to be brave one day, and she has felt braver ever since.

I will be brave all day today. If I feel a little bit scared about something, I won't let that stop me from acting bravely.

TAKING A TIME-OUT CAN HELP WHEN I'VE GOTTEN EMOTIONAL ABOUT SOMETHING.

My mother, dad, and teacher often make me take a time-out when I've misbehaved. I have had zillions of time-outs. Getting quiet when I have behaved inappropriately actually helps me. Most recently I was really upset because my brother got into my colored chalks and broke most of them. I needed them for a special picture I was making for science class. I screamed and threw the remaining chalk at him, and I got a time-out. It didn't seem fair, but it did help me to feel calm.

Taking a time-out gives me a chance to think about what I was doing. Almost every day I do something that isn't very nice. I don't always get a time-out for it, but I always know when I deserved one. Stopping to think before I do anything can help me avoid time-outs. This is good advice to follow, don't you think?

I will not get a single time-out today
if I stop and think before I act.

I WANT TO FEEL MYSELF PART OF THINGS.
–JOANNA FIELD

I'll bet you hope the teacher likes you the best of all the girls in your room! That's the way most of us feel. Adults like to be considered special too. Everybody wants to be an important part of the action. And do you know what? YOU ARE IMPORTANT. YOU ARE SPECIAL! Every one of us is special. Do you know why? Because there is no one exactly like you. There are no two people exactly alike in all the world. Every one of us is needed to make the rest of the world complete.

If you are special, that means your friend Emily is special too. Do you always treat her like you think she is special? Maybe this would be a good thing to do: show the people you care about that you know they are special.

*I will treat my friends and family members the
way I want to be treated today: as a special person!*

FEELING PEACEFUL COMES AND GOES.

Being peaceful means that I feel quiet and not afraid. Lots of times I am not very peaceful. For instance, last week I wondered for three days if Dad would be mad at me for breaking his hammer. I was trying to hang up a picture in my bedroom when I dropped the hammer, and the handle broke off. Every time I thought about what had happened, my stomach tightened up.

When I'm scared that my teacher will think I cheated on the spelling test because I got all the words right, I certainly don't feel peaceful. Sometimes I feel like thoughts are racing through my mind at a hundred miles an hour, and most of them keep me from being quiet.

Mom says I should remember that God will help me handle any problem that comes up. Even the big ones, like when she or Dad are mad at me. When I think about God, I feel more peaceful instantly. Other things that help me feel peaceful are painting, playing the piano, and going for a bike ride.

*If my mind is in a hurry today, I will take time
to do something that makes me feel peaceful.*

IF I WORK HARD FOR WHAT I WANT,
IF I KEEP TRYING AFTER I'VE BEEN TURNED AWAY,
MY DREAMS CAN COME TRUE.
–LISA GUMENICK

Most of the things we want in life require our effort.
For instance, if I want to get good grades in school,
and I do, I have to study really hard. Actually I have
to study harder than my sister. Abby is smart. She is in
the advanced class in almost every subject. When we
compare our homework, I am relieved mine is so much
easier. My grandmother says Abby is gifted academi-
cally. But she is quick to tell me that I am gifted in
many ways too. For instance, I am a natural at the piano. I hardly even have to practice a song to master
it. She says that's unusual.

Something neither Abby nor I is very good at is sports.
We tried out for the softball team but didn't make it.
Abby didn't really care, but I did. All of my friends
made the team. Mom has promised to play catch with
me every night for a week so I can try out again. I
know I can make the team if I really work hard.

I will work on making a dream come true today.

MEETING STRANGERS COMFORTABLY IS A SIGN OF MATURITY.

Have you ever been invited to a birthday party where you didn't know many of the girls and boys and you felt scared to go? It's scary sometimes to meet new people. But if we can remember that these kids are just as scared as we are, we will feel better. When we say hello and they answer back, we begin to feel better. It's kind of magical. And before you know it, you are having fun.

It is good if we can learn how to meet new people because they will always be coming into our lives. A new family may move in next door. New kids will come into our classroom at school. That happens every year a few times. The afterschool program will mix us up with a lot of kids we don't know from all over town. If we decide to look forward to meeting them, our lives will be more fun. We can do it!

If a new girl comes into my room today,
I will try to be the first one to say hello at recess.
I will remember that she might be scared.

IT'S GOOD TO TAKE OUR QUESTIONS TO GOD.

Every time I wonder what I should do or say when a friend does something that upsets me, like when Stephanie hid my coat under hers so I couldn't find it, I can close my eyes and speak softly to God. God can help me respond to a mean act in a way that isn't hurtful. Hurting someone back is usually not the best thing to do.

There are many times I don't know what to do. That is true for everybody. Even my parents get confused. Some dads wonder if they should quit a job. Maybe my mother wants to go to college, but she isn't sure she has time. I heard the teacher say he would like a new car but was afraid it cost too much. Some questions are bigger than others.

*If I wonder what to do today about even a
little thing, I will ask God to give me a suggestion.
Mom says I will be able to feel the answer.*

SHARING SOMETHING PERSONAL CAN BE A GOOD IDEA.

Yesterday my friend Amanda was feeling hurt because she hardly ever gets chosen to play on either team at recess. I felt sad for her and told her about the time the same thing happened to me. It seemed to make her feel better. Sometimes just sharing a little story about ourselves can help someone else feel better.

My big sister says one of the reasons we all have hard experiences is so we can help other people when they have the same kind of experience. She calls sharing something that makes another person feel better getting a turn at being God's special angel. Sad feelings are a part of having a warm and open heart. Sharing these feelings is how people connect with each other: human to human, heart to heart. It's an important part of friendship.

Today I will make room in my friendships to talk about my feelings and to listen to my friends' feelings, heart to heart.

THANKFULNESS CAN BECOME A HABIT.

Moms and dads say we can't be too grateful. They also say we have received many blessings for which to be thankful, blessings we ignore. Let's try to name some of them. Are you reading this page right now? Then you obviously have eyes and a brain that works. Those are two blessings. You picked up this book from wherever it was, which means you have arms that move. You know you will have food to eat today. That's a blessing, for sure. There are kids all around the world who will be hungry all day. And no doubt you have clothes on right now too.

Saying thank you to your dad for waking you up or thanking a big brother for helping you clean the house is good practice. There are lots of opportunities for practicing thankfulness in a day.

*I will write down some of my blessings today
and put the list on the refrigerator.*

FEELING SORRY FOR MYSELF IS OKAY ONCE IN A WHILE.

Sometimes it feels good to feel sorry for yourself. Like the day it was raining and I couldn't go to the playground. Or when my little sister was sick and my dad decided it was better if Betsy didn't come for a sleepover. When something doesn't go as I thought it would, feeling sorry for myself almost makes it easier to accept. Isn't that weird?

Mom says feeling sorry for myself is normal when disappointing things happen. She also says, "Don't make a career out of it." Sometimes, I shift my focus just a little bit, so I can see that things aren't bad. For instance, that rainy day, we ended up having a checkers tournament—it was a blast. And the night my sister was sick, I got to watch a movie, and the next week I had Betsy over. Feeling sorry for myself keeps me from seeing that the best thing generally happens, even though I may not understand it at the time.

*I will try to remember that whatever happens
today is probably for the best. Mom says,
"When life gives you lemons, make lemonade."*

GENEROSITY MAKES AT LEAST
TWO PEOPLE FEEL GOOD.

Sharing my favorite doll with Chelsea is a nice idea. She has lots of sisters and brothers, so she doesn't get as many gifts for her birthday and at holidays as I usually do. Sharing with her shows that I really like having her as a friend. It also shows that I trust her to take good care of my favorite things.

Generosity can be shown in other ways too. I can show a generous spirit with my words, for example. Why not tell Jerrilyn that I really like her? I can be generous in my prayers also. I do this by praying for all the members of my family, all of my friends, my neighbors, even those kids I don't like so very much. Mom says it's the most generous thing I can ever do!

The best thing about being generous is how good it makes me feel. I will remember to be generous in some way today.

MAKING AN APOLOGY WHERE IT'S NEEDED IS A GOOD HABIT TO DEVELOP.

Are you quick to say you are sorry when you've been bossy toward your brother? What about when you push ahead in line at school? Do you apologize then? Lots of girls need to make apologies for talking behind a friend's back. Is this something you've ever done? Did you apologize for it? There are possibly many times every day that you act before thinking, and sometimes that creates a need for an apology.

Learning when to apologize and being willing to do it without being reminded by your teacher or your mom is a sure sign that you're growing up. In time, it will seem natural to say "I'm sorry" and really mean it. And when you are older, you will even be able to stop yourself from doing the very thing you're apologizing for today.

If I need to, I will apologize for my actions today.

LIFE ISN'T ALWAYS FAIR.

My best friend Annie gets invited to every party held by our classmates. I get invited to a few of the parties, but not all of them. Just last week I found out she was going to Leah's party. Leah is the newest girl in our fourth grade class. She moved here from New Jersey. I really don't understand why I was left out, and I secretly wish Annie wouldn't go either. I sometimes feel afraid Annie will end up choosing to be someone else's best friend. Do you understand how I feel?

My dad is famous for saying, "Life isn't always fair." Every time I whine or complain about how a situation has upset me, he says it. I get so tired of his saying this. Mom says he is right though. She told me how she felt about being left out when she was young too. I realized her feelings were just like mine. That made me feel better. I guess Dad is right: Things happen just because they happen. Usually no one intends to hurt your feelings. That's just how life goes, he says.

If something feels unfair today, I will try to remember that's just how life happens sometimes.

"MAY THE FORCE BE WITH YOU."
–*Star Wars*

Did you ever see the movie *Star Wars*? My mom rented it recently. My parents had seen it when they were much younger, and they said it had a good message. Mom popped popcorn and my stepdad made fudge, and then we all sat down together to watch it. The part about "the Force" was really neat. Mom said she always thought of the Force as God. My stepdad said he thought of the Force as a guardian angel smoothing the way for him. I'm not sure what the Force means to me, but in the movie the idea of it made me feel safe. It made the characters seem stronger too.

After the movie, my stepdad wondered what I thought about it. I really haven't decided yet, but I do like the idea that there is a power around me all of the time that can help me. Mom believes we can call the power anything we want. The important thing is to remember that it's there waiting for us to express our need for it.

I will remember that "the Force"
will help me today if I need it.

EVEN THOUGH I'M LEARNING TO DO MORE AND MORE
ON MY OWN, I STILL NEED HELP IN SOME AREAS.

I suppose you think some people never need any help.
For instance, the smartest girl in your room at school
maybe never needs help in reading, even though you
do. Your big brother can reach the top shelf of the
kitchen cabinet, so he never needs help to put the
dishes away. You won't need to stand on the chair to
reach the top shelf in another year or two, either. You
don't need help anymore to tie your shoes, but when
you were little, you did. You can even put your hair
in a ponytail and play softball now.

There's nothing wrong with needing help, though.
Even dads ask for help carrying the garbage cans out
to the street. For sure, most moms can use help when
it is time to fold clean clothes. Being able to help each
other is an important part of our lives. My grandmother believes that's why we are born into families.
She says learning to help one another is the main lesson each of us needs to learn.

I will accept help gracefully when it's offered today.

BEING RUDE IS NEVER A GOOD CHOICE.

Do you know what it means to be rude? It means not answering someone very nicely. Or it may mean not answering the person at all. Like when your mom calls you to dinner and you are busy at your computer and don't answer her—that is being rude.

Adults are sometimes rude to kids perhaps because they are crabby or tired. It never feels very good to be at the receiving end of rude behavior. The opposite of being rude is being considerate of others. All of us can learn from one another. You are never too young to be a good example.

Today I will make choices to be
considerate rather than rude.

GOD INSISTS THAT WE ASK.
–CATHERINE MARSHALL

What are you most uncomfortable about? Do you know what makes me most uncomfortable? It's being afraid. I hate feeling afraid, and there are lots of times when I am afraid. Mother says it would help if I kept the thought of God in my mind more often. She says I can't think of two things at once. There isn't room for fear and God too. If I ask God to stay in my mind, then fear has to leave.

Sometimes fear just seems to come, even when nothing seems to be causing it. And sometimes I forget to ask for help with my fear. But when I do ask my mom or God for help, my fear melts away.

*I will practice putting a picture of God in
my mind today, especially if I am feeling afraid.*

A GOOD ATTITUDE HAS TO BE CULTIVATED JUST LIKE A GARDEN.

Attitude is important. You may have heard your mom or dad say, "You have a bad attitude, young lady!" Maybe you didn't know exactly what that meant, especially when you were young, but you could tell by the tone of their voices that it wasn't good. Being pleasant to all the members of your family is one way of showing a good attitude. This can be done in simple ways, like saying "Good morning" or "How was your day?"

A good attitude means being friendly and warm. It also means expecting good things to happen, not bad things. Families are a great place to practice having a good attitude.

If I can't say something positive or friendly whenever someone calls out to me today, I will say nothing. All day I will have a good attitude.

SHARING SECRETS REQUIRES TRUST.
–KATHY ANDRUS

Don't you love it when a friend shares a secret with you? It makes me feel special when I have been chosen to hear a secret. Knowing something that my friend has told no one else usually means we're special friends.

Secrets can be about many things. A common secret is sharing who we like among the boys. Maybe we share that we miss our dad and wish he would move back home. Pretty often the clothes I wear to school came from a garage sale, but I am afraid to tell that secret to anyone. Mom says it is good to tell at least one other person the secret things that make me uncomfortable. She says my grandmother would keep any secret I needed to tell someone.

*I will tell someone I can really trust about
a secret that is bothering me today.*

PRACTICE IMPROVES EVERY SKILL.

Have you ever wished you were someone else? Perhaps someone in your room at school is really good at reading, a lot better than you. Did you ever wish you were she? There was a girl in my room last year who could broad jump farther than any of the boys. I was really jealous of her. So were all the boys.

It's normal to envy others. That doesn't mean I'm bad or that I don't like myself. Envy tells me the things I should work harder at. Maybe if you read more at home, you could be as good a reader as Delia. Tricia's sister takes piano lessons every week so she can be a better piano player. Practice will make everybody better at anything. How about trying it?

If I want to be better in anything today, I will practice!

"You Are What You Eat!"

My mom has this saying in big, bold, red letters across our refrigerator. She has been dieting for a few months, and she says she doesn't want to forget and absentmindedly start to eat something that isn't on her diet. But Dad says he thinks she has it up there as a message to all of us. He has a sweet tooth, which means he really loves sweets. I have a sweet tooth too. And so did my mom before she started dieting. She claims her sweet tooth is what got her into so much trouble.

Now she works out four times a week and eats carrots every time she wants a snack. She looks a lot different than she did last year. She keeps a picture of herself before she started dieting on the refrigerator right along with the saying. It's a good reminder, she says. She has suggested that I go with her to work out so I can develop good exercise habits while I am still young. It would be fun to spend the time with her, so I think I will. Do you exercise and eat healthy food?

*My mom has a good idea. I will pay
closer attention to what I am eating today.*

LIFE IS PERFECT JUST THE WAY IT IS
AND JUST THE WAY IT IS NOT.
–PEGGY BASSETT

Mom and my stepdad Ted are often telling me "Don't worry." But I still do. I wake up worrying. I worry about getting the states in order on Friday's geography test. I worry about all the multiplication tables. Every Wednesday we have a surprise test that includes some of them. I worry about whether or not Tammy will invite me for another overnight. The last time I went, I had a nightmare and woke up her whole family. Right now I worry about whether or not I'll get invited to Alexandra and Anne's eighth birthday party.

My mind seems to worry about things like this all the time. It is always wondering if I will be included or left out of special activities. I wish I could quit worrying so much.

*How can I stop worrying? Mom says I just
have to practice being okay no matter
what happens. She will help me, she said.*

APOLOGIES MAKE US BETTER PEOPLE.

Did you have to say you were sorry for anything you did yesterday? I did. I promised I would come right home after school, but I stopped at Gretchen's house instead. My dad was mad because I made him late for work. I often have to say I'm sorry. He told me that if I changed my behavior, I wouldn't need to be sorry so often.

It is good to be able to say I am sorry when I've been inconsiderate. It means I realize I've done something wrong. I just wish I could stop myself before I do something wrong. My dad says I don't stop to think first. Maybe I have to start asking myself if what I am thinking of doing is wrong before ever doing it.

❁

It probably won't be easy to think first before doing something today, but I am going to try really hard. If I slip up and hurt someone I love, I can say I'm sorry.

OUR HEARTS SPEAK TO US EVERY MINUTE.

My mom says she can tell what the right thing to do is by listening to her heart. That seems like a strange idea to me. I am not aware of my heart talking. Are you? But she explained it this way: She says her heart speaks by making her feel a certain way. For instance, if she is snotty to a friend, her heart feels some pain. When she goes out of her way to be helpful, her heart feels like it is smiling.

She also says her heart seems to nudge her toward doing the right thing. Very quietly, it urges her to go forward with a good idea. One example she gave me was when she decided to marry my stepfather. He had been really nice to her and my sister and me. He helped paint our house. He often brought groceries over and even fixed dinner as a surprise once in a while. And he made all of us laugh a lot. That was the best. Ever since my dad died, we hadn't laughed very much. She said her heart helped her to know that Jack would make a good husband for her and a good dad for us.

*I will be quiet in order to hear what
my heart is trying to speak to me today.*

LEARNING IS FUN AND NECESSARY.

Everything that happens today can teach me something. When I get washed up for school, I can watch how the soap bubbles up on my arms and takes the dirt away. I can listen for the birds chirping and notice if they are calling to warn their friends that I am walking under their tree. We are studying the sky at school, and I am noticing all the different stages of the moon and how the sun is setting later and later. I'm actually beginning to understand how this world works!

Learning to do arithmetic is hard sometimes, but it helps me when I want to buy candy. Since I have learned to be a good reader, it really is fun to travel by car or bus. It gives me a chance to read all the signs we pass. My mom was really impressed yesterday because I knew the word *authority*. Just to prove I understood its meaning, I used it in a sentence for her. Maybe today would be a good day to write a letter to grandma. I can expand my vocabulary by doing that too.

I will learn so many things if I pay attention to all the sounds I hear and the words I see. The world is an amazing place!

LOOK FOR HAPPINESS: IT'S OFTEN NEARBY.

What makes you happy? Does having your favorite dessert make you happy? How about getting to go to a movie when you thought it was too late? My dad is happy when my sister and I get good report cards. Mom is happy when Dad surprises her with a bouquet of flowers. My teacher seems really happy when our class is very quiet, especially when the principal comes to our room. My friend Melissa is the happiest when her dad comes over for dinner.

All of us feel happy for different reasons. My grandmother says it is often the simple things in life that bring us the most happiness. The simple happy things I noticed after she said this were a hug from my mom, the taste of a crunchy apple, sun sparkling across the water near where I live. I would like to be the kind of person who easily finds happiness all around me.

If grandmother is right, I can be happy every day.

BEING PATIENT IS A SIGN OF GROWING UP.

Waiting for dinner makes me antsy. So does waiting in line at the movies for popcorn, especially when the show has already started. Sometimes Mom gets home late from work, and the rule is that I can't go to a friend's house until she says I can. Waiting then is really hard too.

"Be patient!" That's what I often hear from adults. Maybe it will be easier to be patient when I get older. Right now it seems hard, but I can't make anything happen faster by being antsy. Sometimes it helps to do something to fill the waiting time: play the piano or read a comic book or imagine my next birthday party.

If I find myself having to wait for somebody
or something, I can find a way to be patient.

THE IDEA OF GOD IS DIFFERENT FOR EVERY PERSON.
–ANGELA L. WOZNIAK

Did you know that you can talk to God as often as you want? And even more important, you can picture God any way you want. I have decided that God looks like my grandmother. I can't hear her voice, but I can get a feeling about what she is thinking. I talk to my God when I wake up in the morning before getting out of bed. I ask her to help me be really kind to all my friends and my family too. My grandfather says that people talk to God in their own way. He gets down on his knees beside his bed at night and in the morning. God makes him feel hopeful that he will have a good day.

It is good to ask God for help if you are feeling unsure about something. God can make you courageous right away. Everybody needs to get God's help once in a while.

I will ask God for help today,
especially when I need courage.

THE GREATEST GIFT WE CAN GIVE ONE ANOTHER IS
RAPT ATTENTION TO ONE ANOTHER'S EXISTENCE.
–SUE ATCHLEY EBAUGH

Have you noticed there are times when you can't get anyone to pay attention to you? Maybe you're having a problem with your homework, or you've had a fight with a friend, and you want to talk it over with your mom or dad. Some days they are just too busy with their jobs and all the work around the house to listen. Asking your teacher can sometimes be a good idea, but she gets very busy too.

What do you do when you're bursting inside with the need for someone to talk to? Sometimes I have to say to mom or another adult that it's really important for her to listen, right now. Maybe she doesn't understand how upset I feel until I tell her straight out. And when she says I need to listen to her, whether it's about the next day's schedule or about my aunt who's very sick, I should give her my full attention too.

If I need someone to listen to me, I will ask for that.
In turn, I will listen to those around me.

LIFE IS SOMETIMES PAINFUL.
–THELMA ELLIOTT

What makes you sad? How about when your mom makes you go to bed even though your favorite television show isn't over yet? If I can't find my favorite CD, I am pretty sad. I sometimes suspect my little brother hid it. One of the times I feel saddest is when Dad says he is going to come over after school and take me to dinner, and then he doesn't show up. This has happened two weeks in a row. Why doesn't he even call?

Mom feels sad when her boss isn't very nice to her at work. That would make me sad too, if I were an adult. When my teacher scolds me, I get sad. I think she's like my boss. Being sad happens to all of us, I guess. If I talk to a friend about it, I usually begin to feel better.

*I may get sad about something today,
but that's okay. Sadness goes away.*

OCTOBER

I DON'T HAVE TO BE PERFECT,
BUT I CAN ALWAYS BE GETTING BETTER.

Nobody is perfect all of the time, even Jenny, who never gets into trouble at school. I get jealous of her sometimes. Do you ever feel jealous because a classmate is really good?

Mom says we all make mistakes and they are not such big deals, as long as we are willing to admit them. Pretending we didn't make a mistake, especially one that affects others, is a big deal, like forgetting to close the freezer door so the ice cream melts. That's one of those mistakes I had to apologize for last week. I sure won't make that mistake again.

Making an apology is part of growing up. Making mistakes must be part of growing up too. They go together, according to my mom.

If I make a mistake today, I won't hide behind it.
I'll apologize to whoever is affected by my mistake.

THE THOUGHTS WE CARRY AROUND IN
OUR MINDS INFLUENCE OUR BEHAVIOR.

When I am feeling happy about my experiences, like when Betsy and I have had a great time over at her house, I am willing to be more helpful to my little sister and brother. My happiness makes it easier for me to be nice to them. I'm not sure how the two things are related, but Mom said that what's in our mind more or less takes charge of our behavior. Here is how she explained it to me:

When I play with Matt, I often come home angry and take it out on whoever is close by. Yesterday it was my mom. Matt had called me mean names because I wouldn't play a game by his silly rules, which were wrong, by the way. I left his house really mad, just as his mother was bringing in some cookies for a treat. When Mom asked what was wrong, I stomped up to my room and slammed my door. When we talked about it later, she suggested I spend more time with friends like Betsy.

I will spend more time with people
who make me feel good today.

PRACTICE RANDOM ACTS OF KINDNESS.
-ANONYMOUS

There are so many ways to help. Most of them don't even take very long. For starters, I can help my mother or dad by picking out my own clothes for school. I can gather up all the things I need to put in my backpack. One of the easiest ways to help is by putting my dishes in the sink after I have eaten.

There are lots of ways to help at school too. How about when somebody spills milk at lunch? I can run and get a towel. I can loan Katey a pencil if she has forgotten hers. Last week I saw Zak go up to the new boy in our class and offer to show him where the bathroom was. The more often I do helpful things, the more I am a part of making the world a kind and gentle place.

❧

I can easily find lots of opportunities to help someone else.
I like the idea of making the world a kinder place.

ARGUMENTS ARE A PART OF LIFE,
BUT THEY DON'T HAVE TO BE A BIG PART.

Having a disagreement with a friend is normal, but I hate it when Kristina is mad at me. Even Mom and Hank, my stepdad, disagree sometimes. I guess Brianna's mom and dad disagreed too much because her dad moved out a few weeks ago. Sometimes I could even hear them arguing in their bedroom from my bedroom across the alley. I hope Mom and Hank never argue that much.

My teacher says we disagree because we all see things a bit differently. For instance, yesterday when we were playing softball, I thought I tagged Cody before he got to home plate, but he didn't agree. It's a good thing Mrs. Wilson was watching. She said he was out too. But I think the best thing to do is remember that everybody's point of view matters.

If I start to argue with a friend today,
I will ask myself if I'm truly listening to
her point of view and if I'm clear about mine.

I CAN STAND WHAT I KNOW.
IT'S WHAT I DON'T KNOW THAT FRIGHTENS ME.
–FRANCES NEWTON

Everybody is frightened sometimes. Loud thunder and a bright flash of lightning scares my little sister Hannah. My mom says she is a little bit afraid when she has to drive our brand-new van. Do you ever get afraid when you are trying to cross a busy street on your bike? Maybe that's because you can't see very well around the big tree on the corner. Maybe a car is coming from the other direction. That is probably a good time to be afraid. It can help you be more cautious.

I don't want being scared to keep me from doing something I really want or need to do. I'll just go slow, be brave, and do it anyway. When being scared means I need to be careful, I will pay attention and be careful.

I will take my time in everything
I am doing, so I can keep my fear small.

ONE NEEDS SOMETHING TO BELIEVE IN.
–HANNAH SENESH

Do you ever wonder what God looks like? Mom says he looks different to each of us, but that doesn't mean there is more than one God. I think he looks kind of like Santa Claus, except he doesn't wear a red suit. He looks that way to my friend Janet too. Mom says God looks like a whirling cloud to her. My friend Alicia said she thinks of sunrises, sunsets, and trees as God. I have an African friend who says the tribe her grandmother grew up in worshipped the sun. My Sunday School teacher said God isn't necessarily a man. God could be a woman.

One thing I do know, and that's because my grandmother told me, is this: God loves me regardless of what I do. This love shows itself in beautiful trees, breathtaking sunsets, the warmth of the sun on a sunny day, and a hundred people joined in song. God's love is all around me.

God's love surrounds me.

THE MOST EXHAUSTING THING IN LIFE
IS BEING INSINCERE.
–ANNE MORROW LINDBERGH

Being sincere isn't all that easy on occasion. What do you do, for instance, when a friend asks you if you like her new winter jacket, and you actually don't like the color or the style very much? Gushing over it, saying you love it, isn't being sincere. Can you say something else instead? For instance, that you think the color looks good on her (if it does) or that it looks like it will keep her really warm? Feelings won't get hurt this way, and you won't feel like you have been dishonest.

Responding to friends insincerely makes me feel tired. Mother suggested my conscience gets worn out from insincerity. It's much easier on our minds and on our hearts, she says, if we give honest and loving answers to our friends and siblings.

*Being sincere when I answer
a friend today is a good assignment.*

WE WERE NOT BORN ACCIDENTALLY.

You probably learned in Sunday School or from some adult that everybody has a purpose, or she would not have been born. Everything that happens has a purpose too. Do you know what that means? It is a pretty difficult idea, but here is what it means. Nobody is in this world by accident. Nobody crosses your path today by accident. Everything that happens around us can teach us something. For instance, when Erin's cat got run over it was sad that Snuggles died. His death made all us kids realize how busy our street was. Now we are all more careful when we cross the street.

I like thinking this way. It makes me feel like my life is important and that everyone around me is special. It also helps me look for lessons in what happens at home, at school, and in my neighborhood.

The people and events in my life all have a purpose.
So does my presence in their lives.

CHANGES ARE PART OF BEING ALIVE.

Life is crammed full of changes. Best friends move away, the cat runs off, Mom gets a new boyfriend and then changes her mind about letting me go to the movie with Heather. Some changes are really tiny and not very important. For instance, I get my hair cut in a new style. Maybe Mom and I decide to move my bed to the other wall in the bedroom. One really frequent change is that I outgrow favorite clothes. That's a bummer, when it's a pair of shoes I love.

If nothing changed, it would mean I wasn't even alive, Mrs. Bradley says. What a funny thought that is! I am glad I'm alive. I'm also glad there are things I can totally count on. Like my mom and dad always love me, and I always love to climb into bed at night with a good book. When there are a few important things I can always count on, then I can weather any other changes life brings me.

Changes are like small, surprising bumps on the road, but the people and things I love help me stay on the road.

GOD IS EVERYWHERE EVERY MINUTE OF THE DAY.

Wouldn't it be nice to be able to see God? Maybe you think about God a lot. I do. Maybe even your parents think about God. My best friend's name for God is the Great Spirit. My friend is Indian and has told me a lot about her beliefs. She says when the wind blows into her from the south, north, east or west, each direction brings special strengths. She and I agree we're lucky that God wants to help us in everything we do.

The Great Spirit never goes away. Sometimes friends move away. A parent sometimes has to leave too. Maybe your dad has to move to another city for a while, like Melanie's dad did. Many things can change even when we don't want them to. But we are really lucky that God never changes and never goes away. Ever. If we want to talk to God or the Great Spirit, all we have to do is close our eyes. We will always be listened to.

I can count on God or the Great Spirit
hearing me today if I feel like talking.

SMALL DISAPPOINTMENTS DON'T MEAN I HAVE TO FEEL SORRY FOR MYSELF.

Maybe the birthday present I expected to get didn't come. Or the special bike I asked Santa for wasn't under the tree last year. The baby-sitter was supposed to rent a movie, but she forgot again. So many things can happen that I don't like. But does feeling sorry for myself make it any better?

At first I thought feeling sorry made me feel better. It doesn't change anything, though. When the baby-sitter forgot the movie, I was really disappointed until we got out the Monopoly game and played a huge tournament. Maybe not getting what I want is not as big a deal as I make it.

I am pretty lucky. I just forget that sometimes. Today, even if something disappoints me, I will try to remember that.

EVERYONE IS UNIQUE.

You have probably heard some adult, like your dad or your teacher, say that God created everyone for a purpose. Do you ever wonder what your purpose is? By going to school, making friends, and learning to solve problems, every one of us will figure out our purpose. That's what the adults in my life say.

But if you happen to live next door to a grouchy neighbor or if there is a mean kid down the street, maybe you start to wonder if God really has a purpose for them too. Maybe what you most need to learn is how to stay out of the mean kid's way and not trample on the grouchy neighbor's flowers. Actually, maybe that other person's purpose includes what you need to learn. My mother occasionally has me deliver homemade cookies to the grouchy neighbor. He actually smiled and thanked me last time. I think the world is full of surprises. My grandmother always says, "God works in mysterious ways."

Every person I meet is different and has a purpose.

BEING TRUTHFUL CAN SAVE ME A LOT OF GRIEF.

It is really hard to always tell the truth. When I have done something I promised I would never do again, like pick Mrs. Hardy's roses for my teacher, I am afraid to admit the truth. Even if Mom doesn't know I did it, I do, and it makes me uncomfortable until I finally tell her. What's even worse is that she makes me go over to Mrs. Hardy's house and tell her too.

There is only one way to avoid that kind of yucky feeling: never tell a lie and never do anything I promised I wouldn't do. Some days, no matter how hard I try, I mess up. I guess that's normal, though.

If I am about to tell a lie today, I will think again.
Maybe I can avoid it.

MAKING A DECISION ISN'T ALWAYS EASY.

My dad moved away from our house. My mom said that was a hard decision for him to make. After you think carefully about something, you are ready to make a decision about it, Mom says. I make decisions too. Last year I decided I wanted to take ballet lessons. That meant giving up Saturday afternoons as playtime, which was hard, but I love dancing ballet!

I decided to start waking up 15 minutes earlier than usual–it makes my mornings less rushed and I'm calmer when I head to school. Last summer I decided to read a half hour every day–already I'm a better reader. When I decide to go outside and play instead of watch TV, I feel healthier.

I will make my decisions carefully today.
They will make my day turn out a certain way.

EVERY RELATIONSHIP IS A TEACHER.
–BRENDA M. SCHAEFFER

Do you notice how your friends treat you? Are they polite and generous with their possessions, or do they ignore you sometimes? Does your little brother call you names? It is important to notice how others are treating you because this can be a clue about how you should treat them.

My grandmother says life is like a boomerang. Do you know what a boomerang is? It's a curved stick that returns to you after you have thrown it. How you treat someone comes right back to you in the way they treat you. If you are thoughtful and kind to all the kids in your class, usually they will be kind back to you. If you compliment your little brother, he will be kind in return.

I will notice how my friends and family members treat me today. That will help me see how I'm behaving.

CRYING IS OKAY.

Do you ever start to cry even when you can't think of a single reason for it? That happens to me sometimes. Mom says maybe I had a bad dream even though I can't remember it. I always feel sad when my dad has to cancel our plan to go out for supper. I only see him two times a week. Things can happen in a day that make me feel bad, and crying is a natural reaction. It can make me feel better. Some people even think it washes away the sadness.

My older sister cries at sad movies. Moms cry when their children have been gone a long time and they don't know where. My dad sometimes cries when he hears a beautiful piece of music in church or at a concert. My brother cried when he got dropped from the A team in basketball. Tears are good for all of us. They help move the sadness out of our bodies.

*If I start to cry today, I will just let the tears come.
It is okay to cry, even if I don't know why.*

FIND SOMETHING OF YOUR OWN TO DO.
–SHEILA THOMSEN

Some days I am bored. I have read all my books, most of them two or three times. My Magic Markers are mostly dried up so it's no fun to use them. My best friend Sandra is at her grandmother's for the weekend, so we can't play with her Nintendo game. Dad is cleaning the garage, and my mom isn't here. I don't know where she is. I really hate to be bored!

My teacher says if we are bored it's because we are not using our imagination. Dad says if I am bored I should offer to help him in the garage. Maybe I could make some cookies for our dessert. Maybe I could even fry the potatoes for dinner. Once, after being bored all morning, I wrote a play and acted it out all by myself. It was so fun. Being bored is a decision, according to Dad. There is always something to do.

If I think there is nothing to do today, I will just think harder.

KNOWING GOD ISN'T AS HARD AS IT SOUNDS.

I bet you don't think you know God. I didn't think I knew God either. But my Auntie Maria said all I needed to do was look around me to know God. She said God was everywhere, every minute of the day. Just because we can't see a *godly person* doesn't mean that God isn't present. She says she sees God in every tree she looks at and in every flower, every bird, every sunset, every child, even in grouchy old men.

We took a walk right after she told me this, and she pointed out all the places she knows God lives. She pointed out hundreds of places in just a three-block walk. Wow! When I told Mom what Auntie Maria said, she said she found God most easily in friendly people. She also said that she learned as a child that we could all help God a great deal by our kindnesses to each other. Her church taught that God loves us all, and by being kind to each other, we are helping God do His work. That's a good way of knowing God better because it shows us how God feels all of the time.

I will be really kind to others today
and look for God all around me.

MIRACLES ARE EXPERIENCES
THAT TAKE US BY SURPRISE.

When a huge thunderstorm ends right before your classroom's picnic, do you think that's a miracle? Or if you had counted on going to the zoo with the Brownie troop but had to wait until it quit raining, did you think it was a miracle when the rain stopped just moments before the bus came to pick you up? Running across the street without looking and just barely missing being hit by a car seems like a miracle for sure. But are these really miracles? Or is it just luck when things turn out this way?

Some people say a miracle is when God gets involved and makes something good happen that surprises you. Other people say a miracle is when you discover you can change your mind about something you were really sure about. Like when you are sure you are ugly, and one day you notice how cute you really are. Lots of things seem to count as miracles.

*I will notice all the good things that
happen today. Maybe they are miracles.*

THERE ARE LOTS OF WAYS TO SHOW RESPECT.

Showing respect for others can be done in thousands of ways. Listening and paying attention to my teachers is one example. Picking up the umbrella Mrs. Brown dropped by my fence and taking it to her is another. Asking for seconds on the mashed potatoes at dinner is better than just reaching across the table for them. Holding the door open for an elderly man or woman shows respect too.

One of the easiest ways to show respect is to not interrupt while someone else is talking. I interrupt a lot! I often have to remind myself to wait for my turn to speak. It's not really very difficult to learn to be respectful. It just takes practice.

I will set a good example for my friends today by being respectful at school and on the playground.

MANY FEARS CAN BE EASED IF I TALK ABOUT THEM.

Lots of things scare me just a little bit. For instance, walking down a dark hallway to the bathroom in the middle of the night. Maybe I could ask my mom to put a night light in the hallway. Or maybe I have to go down into the basement to get my pajamas out of the dryer. If the light isn't on, it can seem pretty dark.

Do you hear strange sounds that seem like they're coming from the closet while you're trying to go to sleep? Do you sometimes have to get up and look or call for your mom or dad? It is okay if you do. Every time you check something out that has scared you, you're not as scared the next time it happens. Being scared is nothing to be ashamed of. Even adults are scared once in a while.

I will not be bashful about my fears today.
If something makes me scared, I will say so.

HANDLING YOUR TEMPER TAKES A LOT OF EFFORT.

Occasionally I feel like yelling and throwing my books across the room, particularly when I am doing home-work and can't remember how to do the assignment. When I get mad at my brother, it seems to make me feel better to yell. Mom says it would be productive if I learned other ways to handle my temper besides throwing things and yelling. One of the easiest ways is by talking about my anger to her or my grandmother, who lives with us. Another is by talking to one of my dolls. I can even yell at the doll if it helps. When Mom was young, she loved to go outside and run as fast as she could up and down the street when she was really mad. Eventually this made her the fastest girl on her track team!

Letting my temper push me to be better at some ac-tivity is a good way to handle anger, I think. I like the story Mom told me about running track. Maybe I could try the same thing.

*Doing something constructive with
my anger sounds like a good idea.*

REMEMBER THE SPIRIT INSIDE YOU.

There is something very special inside all of us. Maybe you already know what it is. Have you ever heard of *Spirit*? That is what is inside every person. Even grouchy old Mr. Lynch next door has Spirit. Heidi, my aunt's newborn baby girl, and Dustin, the mean kid across the street, have Spirit too. Every one of us has it.

Do you wonder what Spirit does? I've heard that it helps us be kind to others. It helps us remember that everyone is special. It helps me remember that I am special. I sometimes think of God as the Great Spirit. The Spirit inside of me can talk and listen to the Great Spirit whenever the world around me feels confusing or too hard. This almost always makes me feel better and like I'm not alone.

*I will let my Spirit help me today by
connecting me to the Great Spirit in this world.*

DOING SOMETHING WITH CARE
IS A WAY OF SHOWING LOVE.

No matter what I have to do on a particular day, whether it's go to school, go to grandmother's house, or go to the doctor, I can decide to do it with a pleasant feeling in my heart. Having a warm feeling inside is a choice I can make, according to my mother. It seems like a funny idea, though. How do I choose to feel warm inside? Mom says it all starts with an idea that I can bring into my heart.

I like feeling good. I like treating others in a respectful way. Whenever I am mean to someone, I feel rather sick inside. I am glad I realize now that a lot of what I feel inside is up to me. I will let my mind and heart work together to make me a more caring person.

I can do everything in a caring way if I want to.
I will notice all of the things I can do today to show I care.

HOW I SEE MY WORLD IS DIFFERENT
FROM HOW YOU SEE YOURS.

Have you ever noticed how many times a day you and
a friend feel differently about something? For instance,
I really love to play Scrabble. Finding words to make
from the letters I have chosen is like doing a puzzle.
My friend Robyn doesn't like Scrabble as well as
Pictionary. Mother says our differences are because I
like to read more than Robyn does and she likes art
better than I do. That makes sense.

Most of us don't feel exactly the same way about anything. Miss Lubovitch says that's what makes this such
a fun world. We are like colors in a rainbow, all different. Our differences make us special.

The way I look at a situation is right for me.
Maybe my brother needs to see the same
situation differently. I can be comfortable
with and even enjoy these differences.

HEROES SET EXAMPLES FOR ALL OF US TO FOLLOW.

During fifth grade, Mr. Schmidt talked to our class about the importance of heroes. I wasn't even sure I knew what a hero really was. I had been taught that Abraham Lincoln was a hero for his role in freeing the slaves during the Civil War. And Amelia Earhart was a hero too. She was the first woman to attempt to fly around the world. She never made it but is considered a hero anyway. Heroes are people who do extraordinary things. But Mr. Schmidt said common, ordinary people can be heroes too.

He suggested that we notice the people in our lives who are always available to help others. From his perspective, they are the *real heroes*. That made me think of Mrs. Simons next door. Whenever my mom is sick, which is often, Mrs. Simons brings over some meal she has cooked. I also thought of my grandfather. He never fails to show up when our family needs help with something. Last week we needed help getting Tabby out of the tree. Guess who climbed the ladder?

I may have a chance to be a hero today.

BIRDS SING AFTER A STORM.
–ROSE FITZGERALD KENNEDY

Something may happen today that will make you sad. Maybe your favorite angel fish will die. Or perhaps Samantha will be absent from school today, which means she can't return your *American Girls* book. Losing a glove while walking home from school made me sad last week because my grandmother had just knit me those new gloves to match my winter jacket.

Things happen that make everyone feel sad. If you never felt sad, though, you wouldn't appreciate nearly as much the times you feel like singing. For instance, when my cat died, we had a burial service in the backyard. My friends and I threw glitter and flower petals where we buried her, and I talked of all my fondest memories of our cat. Pretty soon we were all laughing because she had been a pretty funny cat. In the middle of the laughing and my friends' understanding and the beautiful sparkly glitter, I felt happy again.

If something happens that makes me sad today,
I will be on the lookout for something else to sing about.

IT'S ASTONISHING IN THIS WORLD HOW THINGS DON'T
TURN OUT AT ALL THE WAY YOU EXPECT THEM TO.
–AGATHA CHRISTIE

Yesterday I planned on going to my friend's house after school to play with her new computer, but she got
sick, so I had to come home. What a bummer! Mom
said I needed to look for the "silver lining" in my disappointment. I couldn't see it.

But then, an hour later, my big sister came home early
from school and asked me to go to a movie. If I had been
at my friend's house, I would have missed seeing the new
Godzilla movie. I think that was the silver lining!

Adults say there is always something good that can
come out of every disappointment. Sometimes it takes
a while to see it.

*I wonder if there will be some silver linings
in my life today. I will pay close attention.*

THERE IS NO AREA OF PERSONAL CHALLENGE
THAT GOD'S LOVE CANNOT SOLVE.
–MARY KUPFERLE

Problems of all kinds are normal. My mom says that we were born so we could solve problems. That sounds kind of weird, doesn't it? But she's pretty smart. My dad says that's why he married her. She has a good sense of what's important in life.

Having a problem causes me to think, and that's good. It also gives me an opportunity to quietly ask God for help. Using my brains while I pray is a smart response to a problem. For instance, I was really upset with my big brother because he didn't make it to my school play. He kept acting like nothing had happened, so I wasn't sure what to do. I thought about it, silently talked to my guardian angel about it, and then called up my best friend Sara. I ended up writing my brother a letter and telling him all my feelings. The next day he came home from school and took me out for ice cream, and we talked. That really helped.

I will be glad for my problems today because they are making me smart, especially in matters of the heart.

TELLING SOMEONE YOU LOVE THEM IS LIKE
GIVING THEM AN UNEXPECTED GIFT.
–IRIS TIMBERLAKE

Do you ever go up to your mom or dad and say "I love you" for no reason at all? It brings a smile to my mom's face when I do it. She says everybody needs to hear they are loved. She even thinks that kids who pick on smaller kids probably don't get told they are loved very often. If they knew they were loved, they would be nicer to everyone. I wonder if she is right.

I like it when Mom tells me she loves me. I always feel like smiling at everyone after I have gotten a big hug from her.

I will show someone by my actions today that I love her.

TELLING THE TRUTH IS THE RIGHT THING TO DO.

Have you ever pretended you lost your math paper because you didn't want your mom to know you got a failing grade? How did you feel the rest of the day? If you're like me, you were probably afraid she would find out. Whenever I tell a lie, I spend the rest of the day worrying about it. It is just so much easier to tell the truth.

Why does it seem so easy for some people to lie? Jeffrey tells lies all the time. So does Amy. I don't trust either of them because I always think what they tell me isn't the truth, either. There are lots of good reasons for always telling the truth. For one, you won't have to worry about people finding out you lied. And other kids will like you better. Plus you won't disappoint your parents. Finally, it's the right thing to do!

If I begin to tell a lie today, I can stop in the middle of the sentence and tell the truth instead.

November

BE YOURSELF!

Melissa is an excellent reader. She sounds out all the new words without help. Kerry is really good in spelling. She says she doesn't even have to study. My teacher says I will find something I am really good at too. But for now, it doesn't seem I am very good at anything. I sure can't run as fast as Mark. I can't paint as well as Susan. Seth subtracts faster than anyone in our group. I wonder if I will ever really be the best at anything?

Do you ever feel like this? If so, here's what you can do. You can talk over your feelings with one of your parents. I talk to my grandmother when my mom is too busy to listen. She helps me see how really good I am at being me! She says that's all I have to be good at right now, and nobody can do that as well as me. I know your parents would tell you the same thing.

I am really good at being me.
That is very worthwhile and special!

No trumpets sound when the important
decisions of our life are made.
–Agnes DeMille

Making up my mind about who to play with today is
only one of many choices I will make. Beth's birthday
is Saturday and I am invited to her party, which means
I need to choose a gift for her. If her best friend Bryce
is there, I will have to decide if I will talk to her. She
and I had a big fight last week.

When I'm in fifth grade, my parents and I have to decide which school I will go to next year. Mom says we
will visit all three possibilities and ask lots of questions.
Getting a feel for each place and knowing as much as
I can will help me decide. Making any kind of choice
is a big responsibility. I'll make the best decisions if I
am thoughtful about them first.

*When I make decisions, it helps to go with my strongest
feelings and to have as much information as possible.*

QUIET MOMENTS REPLENISH OUR SOULS.
–SUE ATCHLEY EBAUGH

Some days it seems like my mind just won't shut up. Does your mind ever feel like that? It just seems to be talking to me all the time. It tells me I am scared when it is thundering really loud outside the bedroom window. It tells me I am not very smart when I miss a bunch of words on the spelling test. Yesterday it told me I was nobody's friend.

Mother says it is good to tell my mind to just be quiet! She says when my mind seems to be saying things that make me sad or afraid, I should imagine a peaceful picture instead. Sometimes I picture our favorite beach, and I can actually feel the sun and hear the waves. Sometimes I picture Grandmother Sylvia because she is so kind to me. If I picture quiet and peaceful places or people, my mind calms down.

*If my mind starts going a hundred miles an hour,
I'll imagine a peaceful thought, until I can
feel the peacefulness inside me.*

MAKING RULES FOR MYSELF, ALONE, IS QUITE ENOUGH.

You want to be the boss of all your friends, don't you? That's how most of us feel. I hate it when someone else is bossing me around, though, so probably my friends feel this way too. What can be done about this problem? The easiest solution, according to my mother, is for me to be in charge of no one but myself. Of course, she says she is still in charge of me because she is the mom! And that's a mom's right!

Until we are moms or dads, it is best to give up the idea of making rules for anyone else to follow. If you want to have friends, you better let everyone else follow her own rules. Maybe you can take turns once in a while making the rules for everyone else. What a good suggestion!

Although I may suggest my way, I will not try to push my rules on anyone else today.

IT IS OFTEN THE SMALL, SIMPLE
GESTURES IN LIFE THAT REALLY MATTER.

Everyone has a lot to be proud of. For instance, did
you help your parents a little bit this morning before
you went to school? Maybe last night you did the
dishes. Did you give a friend some help in reading a
word that was too difficult for her? Maybe there are
other things you can think of that you feel proud of.
Why not write down two or three?

Mom feels proud when she gets a raise at work. It
means she has worked really hard. Do you get an allowance for doing chores? Some kids do, and when
they start doing more work at home, maybe they get
a raise too. You can feel proud just because you're
able to read this message. It means you care about
making your life better.

*I don't have to do something huge to feel proud. I can feel
proud about saying* please *without being reminded to or
about helping Rebecca with her homework.*

I AM LEARNING HOW TO HELP OTHERS.

Does your mother have a job away from your house? Mine does. Most moms have to work at jobs because food and clothes cost so much. Moms generally want us to have all the things we need and, unless they work, we can't have those things. Does your mom ever ask you for help since she is so busy? Are you willing and eager to help her?

Some kids whine when their mom asks for help. Maybe you have whined a lot in the past, but you don't have to whine anymore. Part of growing up is being willing to help when there is work to be done. Being asked to help is a sign your mom thinks you are growing up. That's a compliment! You can even offer to help before being asked.

I will look for ways to show I am
growing up today. I will offer to help.

WE ALL HAVE BAD HAIR DAYS.

Does it seem like nothing goes the way you want some days? Maybe it starts out with your hair sticking out really funny because you slept on it crooked. Or you counted on wearing a favorite skirt, and the zipper broke when you were getting dressed. But worst of all, you get all the way to school and remember that you left your homework on the kitchen counter.

Mom says I have to learn to "roll with the punches." What a funny picture that makes in my mind! Probably at least one thing will happen every day of my life that I don't like, she says. She also says, "Don't make a mountain out of a mole hill."

I wonder if I can "roll with the punches" today.
I think I will try.

ANGER IS A FAMILIAR FEELING.

Having angry feelings is normal. Sometimes my head begins to hurt because I feel so angry. What kind of things make you angry? Having a fight with a friend over whose turn it is to bat can make a person angry. Getting in trouble for hitting a younger sister who hit you first can make you angry. Being sent to the principal's office for talking back to the teacher can get you pretty upset, especially when you have to take a note home to your parents.

Feeling angry is not much fun. It's hard to think about other things when I am angry. Sometimes I don't hear the teacher call on me to read when I am angry. And I can't eat my lunch because my stomach feels upset with the anger. I have found a few things that help when I'm angry: talking about my feelings, playing a loud song on the piano, or riding my bike really fast. All of these help move the anger right out of my body—and then I feel better.

When something starts to make me angry today, I will think of a way to help move the feeling out of my body.

LAUGHTER CHANGES EVERYTHING.

I love to laugh. Whenever my brother tells a joke, we all laugh, partly because he usually gets the joke all mixed up. I love it when my dad teases me and sings me silly songs. That always makes me laugh and feel loved.

Our teacher makes me laugh sometimes when she gets the twins mixed up. They play a joke on her once in a while by sitting in each other's seat. The whole class laughs then. Laughing makes me feel good all over. Robyn's dad is a doctor, and he says it is really good for us to laugh. Laughing makes our bodies healthier, he says.

Every day something happens that makes me laugh.
I wonder what it will be today?

DEATH COMES TO EVERY LIVING THING.

Have you ever had a pet who died? You probably felt really sad and lonely for your pet for a long time. When my dog Tony got hit by a car and died, I was really upset. It seemed so unfair. He didn't mean to run in front of that car. Having a grandmother or uncle die is really hard to accept too. We don't want to say good-bye to people or animals we love.

It is helpful to remember good things about people and pets who die. Every living thing will die some-day. Death is natural. Flowers wilt and die. Every tree and plant in the forest and in the yard will die even-tually. But the Spirit part of absolutely everything lives forever. Our pets and our grandparents are still alive in Spirit. Sometimes I still hear my grandmother's gentle laughter inside my head, and I still sleep with a stuffed fuzzy bear that Grandma gave me. My Spirit will live forever too.

I will remember that one part of us lives forever.
That is a good thought to have today.

LISTEN CLOSELY—WHAT DO YOU HEAR?

Are you a good listener? Most of us aren't as good as we could be. Mom has to call me to dinner two or three times. Maybe my teacher has to ask the class to quiet down again and again. Some situations can even threaten our lives if we don't listen. For instance, a honking car means get out of the way. If we don't listen for horns and watch for cars, we can be in big trouble!

Learning to listen is like learning anything else. Riding a two-wheeler takes practice. So does listening. But first you have to decide you want to listen. My mother says that God's messages can be compared to gifts, and they always come to her through other people. If she doesn't listen, she will miss them. I don't want that to happen to me.

*I will listen really well today. I may receive
an important gift if I pay attention and listen.*

LETTING GO OF DIFFICULT FEELINGS IS POSSIBLE.

Having feelings of sadness or anger or confusion is pretty normal. Even my parents have these feelings. Keeping any of them too long in my mind can cause me unnecessary trouble, though. I know this very well because staying angry kept me from having a good time at my dad's birthday party. Everybody else laughed a lot, ate big bowls of ice cream and cake, and then went to the drive-in movie. I pouted, refused to get over my anger, and missed out on the whole deal.

Mom suggested that I practice letting go of feelings that keep me from enjoying the activities around me. She says I don't need to deny that I have them, and she even suggested I talk them over with her or some-one else. She told me she has a special way of letting them go. She closes her eyes, pictures whatever feel-ing is troubling her in a balloon, and then lets the balloon float away, over the trees and into the sky. She promised that it works for her every time she tries it. Do you think it sounds like a good idea?

I will feel my fear or my sadness or anger today,
and then let the feeling fly away like a loose balloon.

DISAGREEMENTS ARE PART OF LOVE AND FRIENDSHIP.

Probably at least one time today you will have a disagreement with somebody. Maybe you will be playing a game, and your brother will say you are not following the rules. What do you do then? Sometimes you can ask your teacher or your mom. But what if you are at the park and there's no adult to ask?

That has happened to me. Jessica insisted she was right about how to play Sorry. We ended up playing one round her way and one round my way. Once when we played chess, my dad helped us figure out the rules. Sometimes it is too hard to decide who is right. Mom says I should relax a little about always having to be right. That isn't always easy, but it does seem to help my friendships.

If I have a disagreement today, I will remember that I may be right and I may be wrong. I don't always have to be right.

FEELING JEALOUS OF A FRIEND'S
ACCOMPLISHMENTS IS COMMON.

Do you ever wish you were as smart as the smartest girl in your class? Priscilla is the smartest girl in my class this year. Once in a while I secretly hope she gets a bad grade. My mother said lots of kids envy others in their class. She says adults have this kind of envy too. Learning to be happy for other people's talents is a life-long assignment, she says. When I was in second grade, I really wanted to be as good in math as Molly. The teacher always hung up her paper on the board. Mine never got hung up!

When we look at other kids and wish we were more like them, it's good to remember what is special about us. I can't do math like Molly, but I'm a great singer and I can run fast. Instead of paying so much attention to what others can do, I can notice all the things that I do well.

I am right just the way I am.

HELPING OUT IS PART OF FAMILY LIFE.

Does your mother ever ask you to keep an eye on the baby so that he doesn't fall? Or does your dad maybe ask you to help him rake the yard? Many jobs around the house are easy for you to do. You can clear off the table after dinner. You can clean up the broken cookies from the floor. You can even straighten the blankets on the bed and hang up your clothes. It is important to be responsible for certain jobs around the house. That helps your parents a lot and makes you a special part of the family.

The older you get, the more things you can do to help your mom and dad. You will find that the more responsible you are, the more privileges you'll receive. Some day, you will even get to drive a car! That will be really exciting!

I will help with anything Mom and Dad ask me to do today.
I will show them I am growing up.

BE TRUSTWORTHY!

What does it mean to be trustworthy? It means doing what we say we will do. Like if my friend Monica says she will come over after school so we can write our book reports together, I know she will show up. Or if Dad says, "I'll take you shopping after work," he will. Sometimes people can't do what they said they would, but if they explain what happened, I can still trust them.

Trust is a very important idea. Adults often talk about who they trust. Mr. Hilton, the man next door to us, didn't return my dad's hammer last summer, so my dad doesn't trust him anymore. Adults generally don't stay friends with a person they can't trust. My friends should be able to trust that I'll do what I have said I will do. Being trustworthy is very important. So it's important to check with Mom and Dad before I make any promises.

I will only promise what I am sure I can do today.
I want my classmates and other friends to trust me.

WHO IS GOD? AND WHERE?

My grandfather believes God can be many different things. He thinks God is a force for good in the world who lives in our hearts. He also says that all of the bad things that happen, like wars and tornadoes, are definitely not caused by God. Angry people cause wars, he says, and tornadoes happen because of changes in the atmosphere. I like knowing God doesn't cause wars and tornadoes. If God did, it would make life extremely scary.

My aunt Helene's idea of God is nice too, but it isn't like my grandfather's. She says God is in the forests and the streams and the mountains. When she wants to pray and to feel God, she goes outside and listens for God in the breeze. My grandmother goes to mass nearly every day. She believes that God is found most often in church. She wishes we would all go to church with her. It is nice that God can be many things, I think.

I will look for God in many places today.
If I really want to feel God, I will.

WORRYING NEVER HELPS ANYONE OR ANYTHING.

The way most people worry, you would think it helped them. But it doesn't. Ms. Bird says that worry gives us something to do, but it never solves a problem. Most of the things I worry about never happen, my dad says. I used to worry about flunking first grade, but I didn't. I worried about going to the dentist the first time because I was sure she would hurt me. She didn't.

Sometimes I worry that my parents will get a divorce. I know other kids who worry about this also. Sometimes parents do get divorced, but worrying about that won't help.

It can help to put something else in my mind so there is no room for worrying. Maybe a picture of God or a beautiful sunset or a favorite tree. There is so much natural beauty in this world. That can comfort me and help take away my worries too.

Today I will let my worries go by filling up my mind with the things that make me feel peaceful inside.

CHANGES ARE SELDOM EASY TO ACCEPT.

Have you ever looked forward to going on a field trip at school or to a movie with your mom or dad, only to have the plan get changed? When I'm counting on something and it changes, this can make me feel pretty bad. My mom always says things happen as they should. This means that when a plan gets changed, it is because a different plan needs to happen. I may not understand this. Even adults don't always understand it, but I can learn to believe it and even to look for it.

It wasn't easy when my dad decided he wanted to leave our family. I sure wanted something different to happen. I even prayed that he wouldn't leave. But now that he's gone, I can see that there's a lot less fighting. My mom seems calmer, and the time I do spend with my dad now is extra special. Even though it wasn't my first choice, I can see that maybe this is what needed to happen.

I can learn to feel okay about whatever change happens today. Mom says that growing up means accepting changes and all the feelings that go along with them.

I ALWAYS HAVE TWO LISTS: THINGS
I AM HAPPY ABOUT AND THINGS I'M NOT.
–ANNE ARTHUR

Has your mother ever asked you if you got up on the wrong side of the bed? It's a silly question, but it has an important meaning. It is a question people often ask when someone is behaving rudely or being a grouch. My mood is no secret. When I'm happy, it shows. When I'm not, that shows too. Others can tell right away how I'm feeling. Everything I do shows my mood.

But can I change a bad mood? I sure can! All I have to do is make a decision to act differently. Sometimes putting on my favorite music helps me to do this, or talking with my best friend Betsy on the phone or at school. Like magic, I feel better. The next time I feel like being a grouch, I'll try doing one thing that makes me happy, and it will change my mood.

It never feels very good to be bossy or to pout.
If that is what I start to do today, I will think
about what I can do to feel happier inside.

EVERYONE IS DIFFERENT IN THEIR OWN WAY.

There are three kids in my class at school who I don't like to play with. Julia is one of them. She always bosses us around. When she starts choosing up sides to play kickball, I walk the other way. I don't like playing with the twins, Mark and Mike, either. They always gang up on the smaller kids.

Mom says I don't have to play with people who are mean or unfair, but she says that everyone has something to offer the world. For instance, I don't like to play kickball with Frances, but when she opens her mouth and sings in school or on the playground, it's like diamonds are floating out into the air. That girl can sing!

I will not forget that everyone is important in her own way, even someone I don't like very much.

GUARDIAN ANGELS CAN GIVE US COURAGE.

Rose was chosen for a big part in the school play. The second week of rehearsal she began to doubt that she could learn her lines or sing her solo at all well. She was actually thinking of dropping out. Rose's favorite aunt suggested that she picture a guardian angel around her. The angel could help her with her lines and would always tell her, "Yes, you can do this." This helped Rose so much. She began to enjoy rehearsals and to have fun with her lines and songs.

Whenever a thought comes into your mind that fills you with doubt and makes you afraid, picture a guardian angel over your shoulder. Some people think guardian angels are always around us but we can't see them. But if you think one is there, you can relax because you know she will protect and help you.

I will practice thinking about my guardian angel today.

SOMETIMES WE JUMP TOO QUICKLY TO CONCLUSIONS.

Do you ever feel embarrassed because you yelled at a friend for something you thought she did, only to discover that she hadn't done it at all? Last week, Whitney and I went to the movies. She was sleeping over and didn't remember to bring a sweater with her, so she borrowed my favorite one. Two days later, I wanted to wear the sweater I had loaned Whitney but couldn't find it. I called her up, complaining that she must have left it at the movie theater and that I would never loan her anything again. I even hung up without saying good-bye. When she called back, I wouldn't come to the phone.

That evening I was searching in my dresser for clean pajamas, and guess what I found? My sweater was neatly folded and put away. I asked Mom if she had put it there. She assured me she hadn't. I felt pretty embarrassed. I had not even given Whitney the opportunity to tell me where she put the sweater. I wonder if she is still my best friend? Sometimes my anger comes before I have all the information I need.

Next time, I won't jump to conclusions.

THERE ARE MANY WAYS TO SOLVE DISAGREEMENTS.

Many times I really want a friend to play a game my way. Holly and I argue nearly every time we play cards because neither of us wants to give in. Adults don't always want to give in to their friends either. My dad argues about politics with his brother. Thinking we are right is normal, I guess. But we can't all be right. How do we decide?

Taking turns with a friend is one way of deciding. Also, I can decide that it isn't always so important to do it my way. That is worth trying out, hard as it may be. I can also decide to disagree and still be friends. I've watched my dad and his brother do that.

When I disagree with someone,
there are often several ways to work it out.

Prayer comes in many forms.

Chelsea gets down on her knees to pray. She usually only prays at night, she says. Jennifer goes to church every Sunday and she prays there. When we go to my grandmother's house, we pray before eating, which is called "Saying Grace." My friend Dana, who is Native American, says that when she dances in the powwow, she feels like that's praying. Shana's mom sings in a gospel choir, and Shana says listening to them always gives her goosebumps. That must be a way of praying too.

There is no particular time for praying, according to my mom. We will be listened to whenever we want to pray. The important thing is to have the habit of talking to the Higher Being we believe in. It's like having an invisible friend who will become a better and better friend the more I pray, Mom says.

I will chat, sing, or dance with God today.
Every little talk, song, or dance is like a prayer.

HANGING ON TO ANGER ACCOMPLISHES NOTHING.

I get so mad when someone breaks one of my things! Even when I know the person didn't mean to, like when Katie had a wreck with my bike and broke the horn because she hit a big rock. She skinned her knees badly and was sorry about the horn. I still felt mad at her, though. Being mad stayed with me the whole day. I didn't get over it until I went to sleep.

Being mad is something that happens to everybody. Have you heard your mom yell? You can hear my mom all over the house when she gets mad. Even the principal gets mad when kids run down the hall at school. What is really important is being able to get over being mad. Sometimes yelling helps me get over it, or talking to Susie on the phone, or painting watercolors or playing my horn or writing in my diary. When I get the madness out of me, I feel better.

The next time I feel mad about something,
I will find a way to express it rather than hold on to it.

PEOPLE NEED JOY. QUITE AS MUCH AS CLOTHING.
–MARTHA COLLIER GRAHAM

I love going to the park with my friend Emily. We laugh when we race each other to the slide. We see who can pump the highest on the swings. Even when she pushes higher than I can go, I am happy and full of joy. It's so much fun to have a friend to go to the park with. Making sand castles together is one of the other things we like best.

Another thing I really love is making cookies at my grandmother's house. She never complains when I get flour on the floor, and she always has every ingredient we need for almost any kind of cookie. Last week we made peanut butter cookies, her favorite.

After the cookie making is done, she often tells me stories from her childhood. We look at her picture albums too. I love to imagine that she and I were girlfriends when she was young. I would have had as much fun with her as I do with Emily.

I will look for all of the reasons to feel joy today.

MOMENTS OF HAPPINESS CAN BE FOUND EVERY DAY.

On days I have plans to go to the zoo or to sleep over with a friend, I feel really happy. Mom says it's because I have something to look forward to that I know will be fun. But actually, every day offers me activities that can be fun if I think about them that way. Even just sitting under the big tree in the backyard can be fun if I watch very closely for all the little insects walking through the grass. They don't even know I've noticed them. It's amazing how ants form lines: I like to imagine them talking to each other.

Even if I don't have special plans, every day can surprise me with special moments.

I will look for moments of happiness today—
there is no predicting when it will happen,
so I will open my heart and be ready.

Hope means help is always available.

Most kids hope for lots of things. At my birthday, I hoped for a new bike. I got it too! My brother Caleb hoped for a horse last Christmas, but he was disappointed. Of course, he hopes for one every year, and we wouldn't even have a place to put it. Even my mom hopes for certain things. She hopes her sister gets well soon.

Hoping for things to be a certain way is one kind of hope, but there are other kinds too. My aunt told me that hope is like believing in God or the stars or some force greater and more powerful than myself. It means I can trust that I will always be okay no matter what happens in my life, because I am not alone. Having hope helps me not be so worried.

Today, hope will connect me with all
that is good and beautiful in this world.
No matter what happens, I will be okay.

GETTING YOUR FEELINGS HURT
IS AN EVERYDAY OCCURRENCE.

Everyone gets her feelings hurt. Even moms and dads
and teachers and grandparents get their feelings hurt.
When I'm treated meanly or I'm not included in a
game, my feelings get hurt. Did you ever cause a
friend to feel hurt? If you did, what could you do about
it? Telling someone you are sorry for having said something mean is a nice gesture. Also, making sure you
are more considerate in the future is even better.

When someone hurts my feelings, what can I do about
it? Maybe I can say I'm feeling hurt to that person. Or
maybe I can just quietly talk to myself about it, maybe
even ask my mother to comfort me and help me feel
better.

*If I feel left out today or if someone yells at me,
I will remember that I hurt people's feelings too,
once in a while. And then I'll go on and
talk to whoever I need to about my feelings.*

DECEMBER

TELLING LIES DOESN'T REALLY SOLVE PROBLEMS.

When people are afraid of getting into trouble for a mistake, they may tell a lie about it. I have a friend who told her mother she lost her allowance out of her pocket when she really spent all the money on candy and gum. At first, she bragged about all the candy, but I could tell she was worried her mom would find out.

Telling a lie causes everyone to worry a little bit. Even moms and dads and teachers and neighbors and grandparents feel worried when they tell a lie. It's a good thing lying upsets us a little because it helps us remember to tell the truth. Knowing that everyone starts to lie once in a while helps me not feel so bad about the lies I start to tell.

I hope I can stop myself before I finish a lie today.

EVERYBODY'S A STUDENT—THERE IS
SO MUCH TO LEARN ABOUT THE WORLD.

When I started school, everything seemed pretty hard. If somebody in the class already knew how to read, it made me afraid that I would never catch up. I remember that Tonya already knew how to add and subtract. Wow! Of course, she has an older sister. Dad said her sister probably taught her.

Every day, I have a chance to learn something new. Actually, that makes going to school really fun. By the end of first grade, I knew lots more than I knew in kindergarten. At the end of this year, just think how much I will know . . . stuff about the stars in the universe, the history of the country, and how the clouds make rain. I live in an amazing world, and there is so much to learn about how it works. It looks like I will have years and years of learning ahead.

I have a lot to learn. I love learning about the world I live in.

FEAR CAN ENTER MY MIND SO EASILY.

I had to wait for my dad to pick me up from school yesterday. He was running late and I got cold waiting by the school fence. I had a dentist's appointment. I got scared thinking about the dentist. Sometimes when I have to wait for a certain thing to happen, my mind starts imagining bad things. Waiting can be hard that way. When Dad did show up, I talked to him. He said I could imagine the dentist having very kind hands. I could sing songs in my head while my teeth were getting cleaned.

It's fun knowing I can be in charge of whatever is in my mind. Dad's ideas really helped—my time with the dentist wasn't as scary as I imagined. And I felt good when it was over.

*I will try an experiment today: if fear creeps in,
I will change my mind's picture to happier scenes.*

Being wrong isn't being bad.

Do you feel bad when you make a mistake? Most people do. But Mom says people aren't perfect. Only God is perfect. She says God loves us whether we make mistakes or not. Have you ever noticed an adult make a mistake? They usually seem embarrassed.

Mistakes show us we still have a lot to learn. That is good, really. Admitting a mistake shows people around us that we are willing to learn. It shows them we have a good attitude.

If I make a mistake today, I'll show that I have a good attitude about it. I will look for what I can learn from it.

PLANT AND NURTURE HAPPINESS LIKE A SEED.

No one manages to stay happy all of the time. My grandmother gets mad when the neighbor's dog digs up her flowers. Once I even saw her throw a rock at him. Boy, was I surprised. She almost hit him, too! I get mad pretty often at my older brother. He teases me all of the time. Mom says I should just ignore him. He does it in fun, but it's not very much fun for me!

The worst part about not being happy is missing out on some fun. When my mind is filled with anger, it can't think of anything else. I have noticed that my teacher hardly ever seems unhappy. Even when the class is acting crazy, she is stern for a minute and then pleasant again.

I am going to do an experiment today.
I am going to try being pleasant about everything.
I bet I will have a great day.

WHAT HAPPENS WHEN I DIE?

Sometimes I worry about dying. I always say a prayer when I go to bed at night for protection. My grandfather died last year. I think he is in Heaven. My mother thinks so too. She said I will get to see him again one day. I guess that means after I die. Mom says a lot of our family will be there by that time.

Jessica's cat died last week. Do you think cats go to Heaven? We buried Tabby in Jessica's backyard. I wonder, will it get to Heaven? My Sunday School teacher says just the Spirit goes to Heaven. The body stays in the casket in the ground. There must be a lot of Spirits up there. I wonder what they do all day?

I will think about my Spirit today. It will last forever.

ONCE CONFLICT HAS ARISEN, WE ARE KIDDING
OURSELVES IF WE THINK IT CAN BE IGNORED.
–LINDA RIEBEL

Hearing people argue or being involved in my own arguments can be very upsetting. When my dad gets home late from playing ball, my mom yells at him. When they fight, it scares me, and it happens a lot. When I came home late from Sandy's yesterday, my mom got mad at me too. That scared me a little also because she got really red in the face. Even listening to an argument or being yelled at by someone can be upsetting.

When I was really young, I got sick often because the people in my family yelled a lot. Even when I wasn't the one getting yelled at, I would get a sick feeling in my stomach or my head. I'm not going to stick around today if others are beginning to argue. And if they're mad at me, I'll ask God to help me listen, and then I'll go outside or to my room.

*I don't have to become part of an argument if it makes
me upset today. I can carve out a little peacefulness
for myself by going to my room or going outside.*

FIGHTING IS SOMETIMES A PART OF LIFE.

Everybody fights with somebody. Mom fights with Dad, particularly when he doesn't come home for supper on time. She yells at me too when I don't do my chores after school. She says she needs to count on me to carry out the trash without being reminded. I fight with Jordan when he throws my ball so far that I can't find it. He's stronger than I was at his age! I can hear the neighbors fighting sometimes too. It seems like they fight a lot.

It's normal to disagree about some things, my teacher says. Each of us has our own idea about how things should be. Usually we think everyone else is wrong too! Learning to let things be how someone else wants them to be is okay. I don't have to get my way all the time. No one gets that. Not even Mom.

*If I start to fight today, I will stop and
ask myself if my idea is the only one.*

HOPE CAN CHANGE HOW A SITUATION LOOKS.

Do you worry over big and little things? I do. Mom says I worry way too much. Yesterday I worried about the reading lesson. There were lots of new words in it. I worried about my fish too. I was afraid he would die while I was at school. Some days I worry about my mom at her job. Last week she was upset because her boss corrected her in front of her friends. I know how she felt. My teacher corrects me lots too.

If I feel some worry starting to come into my mind, I can think of an angel. That's what my Aunt Sarah does. Then I give the angel some of my worries. I ask the angel to watch over my fish while I'm at school, which helps me feel calmer. Having a picture of an angel in my mind doesn't leave so much room for worry pictures.

I will keep hopeful pictures in my mind today.
If I need or want to, I can ask an angel for help.

Privileges come with responsibility.

It is not unusual to want to be liked by the teacher. I think I know who she likes a lot by who she calls on. Emma always gets called on to clean the boards. Does that mean she is the "teacher's pet"? Maybe it just means she does the best job. After all, the teacher wants to make sure the boards are really clean before she goes home every day.

If you want to be noticed by the teacher and called on to do special things, like taking a message down to the principal, you need to show her you can be counted on to do them carefully. It is always up to each of us if we want to have special privileges. We have to earn them.

I will make sure I show my responsible side at school today.

GOD'S PRESENCE CAN HELP US BE BRAVE.

People mention God a lot. You hear about God at church. Sometimes at school too. Some of your friends say prayers to God before they go to sleep at night and even before they eat a meal. Do you sometimes say a special prayer when you are feeling afraid about something? I do. I say something like this: "Dear God, help me to have courage right now. Help me remember that You are always here to help me."

Asking God for help–any time, any place–always makes me feel a little bit more relaxed. God never goes away. God is always waiting to help me even if I don't know exactly who God is or what God looks like. No one else knows how God looks either. That's what I read in a book from the library. My mom thinks God looks like a beautiful angel. I like that idea. I think God can look however I imagine.

I will ask God for help when I feel even a little bit afraid.

FEELING SORRY FOR YOURSELF
JUST HAPPENS FROM TIME TO TIME.

Sometimes I just feel sorry for myself. Is that so bad? My mother reminds me I have so many things to be happy about: I have a bed to sleep in with plenty of blankets and a pillow. I have clothes in the closet. And I have friends who like me and a family who loves me. With all of this, I wonder why I feel sorry for myself sometimes?

My Uncle Joe says it's normal to wish for more than you have. His wishes are what motivate him to work hard, he says. My aunt says if she has a big disappointment, she gives herself one day to feel sorry for herself. Then she picks herself up and moves on. I like this idea. When I'm done feeling sorry for myself, I remember that feeling good about my friends or putting my tooth under the pillow for the tooth fairy is much more fun.

*If I start feeling sorry for myself, I'll begin
thinking of all the reasons I have to smile.
The first one might be that my dad really likes me.*

MY MIND IS ALWAYS CHATTERING TO ME.

What idea do you have in your mind right this minute? Are you thinking about these very words you are reading? Sometimes I read words but have my mind on the movie I saw last Saturday or maybe on the dessert I know Mom made for dinner. Then I don't know what I read. When that happens in math class, I don't learn how to do a new kind of problem. Keeping my mind on what is in front of me can be pretty hard.

Sometimes if my mind keeps wandering, I write a note to myself to remember to think about these things later. Sometimes it helps just to take a deep breath and remind myself to pay attention. I get so much more out of whatever I'm doing or learning right now if I give it my full attention.

*I can quiet my mind and concentrate on what
I most need to learn or think about right now.*

HAVING HATE IN YOUR HEART
DOESN'T FEEL VERY GOOD.

I sometimes get so mad at my dad's wife that I think I hate her. And then a little bit later, I feel bad for having this feeling. Mrs. Silver, my teacher, says that it's not okay to hate anyone, especially members of our family. Dad says that too. What about when Sherry, Dad's wife, changes her mind and says that I can't go to Julie's house for a sleep-over?

When the word hate slips out of my mouth, what I'm really talking about is anger, really big anger. It's much better to say, "I'm angry at you." I can be angry at someone and still honor the basic love between us. This may sound hard to do, but I have heard my dad say sometimes that he loves me but not how I am acting. That is something I can learn to say too. I have many opportunities to practice this with William, my youngest brother.

I will be more like my dad today. If somebody is mean to me, I will try to like her even when I don't like what she did.

YOU DON'T HAVE TO SEEK GOD IN CHURCH.
I FIND GOD WITHIN MY HEART.
–SANDRA LAMBERSON

Do you sometimes wonder what God looks like and where God is? No one I know has actually seen God, but everyone has an idea of what God looks like. I used to think God looked a little like Santa. My friend Molly is sure God looks like an angel. She even says she saw God. Mom thinks God is a really bright light that shines everywhere. Her sister says she sees God all over in Mother Nature.

What counts is asking God for help when I am scared or lonely. Talking to someone who I can't really see may sound silly, but I don't have to talk out loud. I can talk just in my mind. God will hear me and I will feel so much better.

*I will talk to God today if I feel scared
or confused. God will hear me. I don't have
to be in church or temple to talk to God.*

WHENEVER I AM BLAMING SOMEONE ELSE,
I FIND THAT I AM JUST AVOIDING MY
OWN FEELINGS OF ANGER OR SADNESS.
–RUTH CASEY

When I can't find my left shoe and it is time for the school bus, I really want to yell at someone. "Who hid my shoe?" When I can't find my hairbrush, I really hope to discover my older sister using it. I always want to blame someone for losing whatever I can't find. If I leave my lunch box on the kitchen table, I want to blame my mom for not handing it to me. And if I miss lots of words on the spelling test, maybe I want to blame my parents for not practicing more with me.

Part of growing up is learning it never helps to blame others for what happens to me. When I realized how disappointed I was about my spelling test, I set up a practice schedule for the next week and practiced with my best friend. That was a lot more constructive than pointing my finger somewhere else.

I will not blame Mom or my sister or the dog
for anything that happens to me today.
Instead, I will change the things I can change.

New friends can be like unexpected desserts.

Kristy is my best friend, and I feel lucky to have her. I can always count on her to play with me, at home and at school. But sometimes best friends move away. That happened to me when I was in kindergarten. Holly was my best friend then, and she moved to Illinois. I felt pretty sad. Mom let me call Holly on the phone a few times, but that wasn't the same as having her to play with.

How do you make a new best friend? When I asked Mom, she told me to notice who likes to do the things I like to do. Best friends usually have a lot in common. Sometimes having several good friends can be as good as having one best friend. And sometimes a good friend gradually grows into a best friend.

Even if my best friend is still in my room
at school, I can have other good friends too.

Getting mad sometimes is okay.

It's not unusual for people to get really mad occasionally. In fact, it would be unusual if you never got mad. Maybe your brother breaks your favorite barrette. Or your mom decides you can't go over to a friend's house for cookies, and you are starving! Maybe you don't even know why you are mad. That's how it happens for me sometimes. I just wake up that way, and the world better watch out! All I want to do is yell mean things at everyone. But when I make that choice, I don't feel one bit better.

Mom says I need to figure out how to have my feelings without making life miserable for others. She suggests I think about things to do instead of yelling at her or my brother. She said she sometimes chooses to sit quietly with her feelings a while and then she pictures them floating away. Another thing she does is make a list of things she is really happy about. Sometimes it helps me to just go outside and play a while.

I will try something new if I feel
some madness coming on today.

BEING ABLE TO THINK IS ONE OF MY SPECIAL GIFTS.

There is so much to think about! For instance, I have to think about what to wear to school. I have to think of the right answers to all of the questions the teacher asks. I have to think about who to invite to sleep over. Mom said I could ask two friends. I have to think about which book to write my book report on. I have to think about not saying the mean things I said yesterday to my brother anymore. Life feels complicated sometimes with all of this thinking.

There are lots of other things to think about too. Sometimes I think about the other planets. Do you suppose people live there also? In small ways and big ways, my mind is always at work. There is so much to wonder about and figure out in this world—I'm glad to have a mind that works.

Even when life feels complicated, I can appreciate how my mind works and how much I am learning.

I ALWAYS FEEL SORRY FOR PEOPLE WHO THINK MORE
ABOUT A RAINY DAY AHEAD THAN SUNSHINE TODAY.
–RAE FOLEY

How often do you worry? You're lucky if you don't
worry very often. My dad calls my mom a worrywart
because she worries about everything. *Worrywart* is a
funny word, isn't it? Mom even worries about my spelling tests! I know she worries a lot about my brother and
me when we are at the park. Worrying keeps her from
having fun with my dad and her friends.

I don't like to worry. It ruins whatever I'm doing. Mr.
Sylvester, my third grade teacher, said worry means
we aren't trusting that everything will work out okay.
That's what my dad says too. He also says people have
all different ways of finding that trust. Some people
walk out into nature and notice a beautiful sunset, and
that helps them trust that all is okay. Some people pray,
and that helps them believe everything will be okay.
Sometimes a hug from my mom helps me to trust that
everything is going to be okay.

*If I worry today, I will think about what helps me to believe
our world is a good place. That way I'll always be okay.*

My mistakes can teach me.

Everybody makes mistakes. According to my teacher, some mistakes are more serious than others. For instance, if I forget to bring back my permission slip, I might not get to go on a field trip. But if I miss one or two words on the spelling test on Wednesday, I can still study for Friday's test.

I had a big project due last week, but I didn't tell my mom until the last day. I had to stay up late working on it, and we didn't have all the supplies I needed, and my mom was upset with me. It was a mistake to wait until the last minute. I didn't get as good a grade as I know I could have. Next time I will tell my mom and get started at least a couple of days ahead! I guess some mistakes teach us important lessons.

I may make a mistake today, but I can learn from it.

RESPECT OTHERS!

Being respectful is not a very hard thing to do, but sometimes I just don't make the effort. Every time someone speaks to me I have an opportunity to be respectful. For instance, I can smile when spoken to. I can listen and answer in a friendly voice if someone asks me a question. I can say *please* and *thank you* at appropriate times.

Opportunities for being considerate and respectful happen all of the time. Any minute another person is present in my life I have such opportunities. I'm going to try to handle most experiences in a friendly voice. The kinder I am, the kinder others will be too.

*I will show my respect to the
people I see and talk with today.*

OUR PROBLEMS CAN BE THE
GREAT SPIRIT'S WAY TO HELP US.

My family has a lot of problems. My father lost his job about a month ago and hasn't been able to find another one. My mother has been very sick for the last few days, and I am worried she might die. Jacob, my oldest brother, has been in trouble at school so many times that he may get kicked out. My dad says if he does, he will have to find another place to live.

I am almost afraid to get out of bed in the morning because so many things have gone wrong at our house. My grandmother came down from the reservation recently to help my mother out. She told me that all of my problems could be resolved by the Great Spirit if only I believed in the power the Great Spirit had. She also said that it may take a while for Dad to get another job and for Mom to feel better. But she promised me that if I asked the Great Spirit to take away my worries, they would leave sooner than I expected. I wonder if the Great Spirit can help Jacob too?

I will ask the Great Spirit for help today,
no matter what kind of problem I am having.

December
· 24 ·

THERE IS NO HEALING WITHOUT FORGIVENESS.
–HELEN CASEY

Forgiveness is a difficult idea for many kids my age.
When somebody lets me down, it can take me a while
before I'm ready to forgive.

Last week my dad forgot to come to my school program. He had promised he would be there, and I kept
watching for him. When he got home that night, he
said he was sorry. It made me feel better, but I was
still sad he missed hearing me sing *Amazing Grace*. He
asked me to sing it just for him, but I was too upset
and mad at him. The next night, he asked again and
when I sang it, he had tears in his eyes. I could see
how much he loved me, and my heart opened and I
felt ready to forgive him.

My Aunt Karen says that asking for forgiveness can
heal broken relationships. Do you understand what
she means?

When someone asks, "Will you forgive me?"
I can try to open my heart to forgiveness.

"CONSIDER YOURSELF PART OF THE FAMILY . . ."

My grandfather often talks about being considerate of others. He says it's a sign of a warm and wise heart. I can be considerate by offering to help my teacher pick up the pencils that fell off her desk. I can stop by Sara's house after school and ask her mother if I should bring work home for Sara, who is sick with the flu. I can set the table for dinner without even being asked.

My grandfather would rather I treat him and everyone in our family with kindness and consideration than spend my allowance on his birthday gift. He says it makes our home a happier one and our family stronger and more loving.

*Today I will open up my heart and do something
kind and considerate. I will make my family
and my friendships warmer and happier.*

IT IS HEALTHIER TO SEE THE GOOD POINTS OF OTHERS.
–FRANCOISE SAGAN

My younger brother often makes lots of noisy engine sounds when he's playing with his trucks. This can really get to me. He also sometimes tries to start fights with me by making faces, grabbing at my arm or taunting me.

Often all I can see is that my little brother is Trouble with a capital T. It's harder to also notice how much he wants to hug me and tell me a story when I've been gone overnight. On the night I burst into tears because I lost my student council election, he hugged me and offered to give me his soccer trophy.

It's really easy to notice the faults of people in our family. But it's important to pay attention to the loving gestures that are meant just for us. That's the way to open up our hearts to give and receive more love.

I will open up my heart and eyes by appreciating kind gestures that come my way today.

EXPERIENCE IS A GOOD TEACHER.
–MINNA ANTRIM

I wasn't sure if I'd like swimming or not. So I joined the swim team but ended up in tears at the end of my first swim meet. After talking it over with my mom, I decided to keep going to swim practice because I really like swimming with my friends. I decided not to go to the meets—I simply didn't enjoy that kind of competition, although I do love skating competitions. My mom reminded me that in the future, if I changed my mind, I could always try a meet again.

I'm learning what I love through experiences. It's important to try activities and see which ones fit me and which ones don't. It usually helps to talk this over with my mom, dad, or another grownup.

Today I will let experience teach me more
about the world I live in and more about myself.

LET THE LIGHT OF LOVE OUTSHINE
YOUR DARK STREAK TODAY.

Have you said mean things to your best friend? Did you feel guilty about it afterwards? Have you ever called your mom a bad name, and then when you calmed down, you felt terrible about it? Sometimes when I feel hurt, disappointed, or angry, it is easy to lash out and say or do mean things.

Being mean doesn't feel very good in the long run. I learned that it's better to talk about my hurt and angry feelings. It's like shining a flashlight into a dark space. When I see what's really there, I can see my mean gesture and apologize for it and start talking about what the deeper problem is.

Today I will let the light shine on any mean streak of mine so I can find what's underneath it.

ADMITTING A MISTAKE MAKES ME MORE HUMAN THAN PRETENDING TO BE PERFECT.

When I've done something I know I shouldn't have, like when I pretended to lose a note from my teacher about misbehaving, then I usually feel guilty. Sometimes I try to brush away guilt feelings, but they don't really go away. In fact, when I finally did give that note to my mom, I was nervous but also really relieved.

Another time I felt guilty recently was when I talked my friend Anna into hiding from Jennifer so we didn't have to play with her. I know what I did hurt Jennifer's feelings because if she had done it to me, I would have been hurt. Later, when I told Jennifer I was sorry, she hugged me and we both felt better. Both times, when I admitted I had done something wrong, I definitely felt better, but it wasn't easy.

Today I will listen to any twinges of guilt I feel.
I'll let them teach me to be more honest or to make amends.

NATURE'S BEAUTY SURROUNDS US.

My dad started taking me camping when I was only six years old–he's wild about trees and campfires and waking up with the birds. On summer nights we sit in the backyard and he points out all the constellations. Often he takes me and my friends on hikes to the neighborhood bird sanctuary: he knows the names of all sorts of birds and wildflowers. What I've learned from him is how much there is to notice and love in nature.

There is always something going on around us in the sky, in the trees, and in the flowers and grasses coming from the earth. When I notice these things, my day feels richer. It's as if nature's beauty and aliveness enters me, comforting me or encouraging me. I notice how much strength I feel from nature's gifts–from my special willow tree or my favorite purple irises– and I'm grateful to have learned this from my Dad.

Nature's strength and beauty are forces that
are always there waiting for me to lean on them.

MORE WORK MEANS I'M GROWING UP.

As I get older, parents and other adults are starting to ask me to do more chores and take on more responsibility. I don't know if I'm glad or if I dread doing grownup work. Some kids are both glad and mad at the same time. My friend Hayley has to sweep the kitchen floor after dinner every night. She complains that it's too hard, but I can see she kind of likes having a big job. Her brother's job is a lot smaller—all he does is carry the dishes to the sink. I think Hayley's job makes her feel important even though she likes to complain about it.

Carrying out the trash, watching the chicken fry so it doesn't burn, and putting the clothes in the dryer are all jobs I've done this week for Heather, my stepmom. My jobs are changing just like I'm changing. By the time I go away to college, I will know how to take care of myself.

I will do my jobs cheerfully today.
My jobs are training me to be independent.